Praise for

Touch My Tears is a significant and moving addition to the record of Choctaw heritage; accessible and entertaining. This fine collection of tales is invaluable for the insights it provides into the heart of a unique Native American culture.

Brock Thoene, co-author of *The Jerusalem Chronicles*

This book is a milestone of fictional and historical Choctaw storytelling that exemplifies the value of Native knowledge through literary arts. This deeply moving and significant collection will hopefully generate a paradigm shift in written expression of the Native American experience.

Keevin Lewis, Museum Programs Outreach Coordinator, National Museum of the American Indian, Smithsonian

A strong representation of the Choctaw Nation and Native people as a whole, *Touch My Tears* presents a time period fading in American history. You did not learn these things in school. But you can now.

Susan Feller, president of the Association of Tribal Archives, Libraries, and Museums

Through the tears of the Choctaw, these authors allow us to see the sunrise, the new beginnings. They take us with them on an unforgettable journey. Of course, these authors aren't writing about strangers or simply information they researched. They wrote about their families, their ancestors, and their own history. That makes all the difference. They brought their ancestors' passion to life for us to live with them. They honor them and us in this wonderful, yet tragic odyssey of an entire people by making it personal.

Fred St Laurent, CEO of The Book Club Network, Inc.

This book reflects the joining of courage and endurance that defines a great nation. I cried in many places, sometimes it seemed more than they cried for themselves.

Lisa Reed, editor of the *Biskinik*,
Official Publication of the Choctaw Nation

Touch My Tears is a heart-wrenching collection of stories in which Choctaw people of the 1830s describe their desperate struggle to survive after removal from their ancestral lands in Mississippi. Almost two centuries later, their voices still convey the sense of betrayal and pain that followed the Treaty of Dancing Rabbit Creek. This outstanding collection was assembled and edited by Sarah Elisabeth Sawyer, who is a Choctaw descendent, and her work allows new generations to glimpse one of the most tragic chapters of American history.

Scott Tompkins, editor, instructor at
Youth With A Mission's University of the Nations

These authors share stories of the Choctaws who were forced from their homes by the desire of some white leaders to expand westward. It makes me stop and think about injustice, and pray that we all will look to the past so as not to make similar mistakes in the future. At the same time, this book is a testimony to people who embraced their new home, found ways to survive, and preserved the Choctaw Nation.

Joan Hall, freelance writer at JoanHallWrites.com

As I child, I learned that Jesus loved all the children of the world—red, yellow, black, and white. I knew about white, because I was one. But I often wondered what it would be like to be from a different race and culture. With the *Touch My Tears* stories, I have a wonderful glimpse into a world that otherwise I could never know.

Frank Ball, author of
Eyewitness: The Life of Christ Told in One Story

Touch My Tears is exactly what a reader will do when reading these stories—they will be touching their own tears. I had tears of sadness for what families went through, and then afterwards I had tears of hope because even through all of the trials that the tribes went through—we are still here.

Lorie Robins, Chickasaw Storyteller

As well as the Plains and Prairie Tribes are known for their mastery of painting and dance, the Choctaws may well go down in history for their remarkable ability to blend their rich oral and written traditions. In the tradition of Choctaw writers such as J.L. McDonald and Peter Pitchlynn in the nineteenth century, Muriel Wright and Louis Owens in the twentieth, and D.L. Birchfield and LeAnne Howe in the twenty-first, the writers in this anthology demonstrate their versatility in the language arts. No tribe has more seamlessly assimilated the English language than the Choctaws. Read these stories and marvel at their quality. They have the multiple capabilities to inspire you, to entertain you, and to educate you. *Ilvppa holisso nan anoli achukma!* These stories are good!

Phillip Carroll Morgan, author of *The Fork-in-the-Road Indian Poetry Store* and *Who Shall Gainsay Our Decision? Choctaw Literary Nationalism in the Nineteenth Century*

Beautiful stories indeed! To know where we came from is to know who we are. It is through stories that our children will remember our ancestors. Languages and traditions are important.

Stella Dyer Long, Traditional Choctaw Storyteller

Touch My Tears

Tales from the Trail of Tears

SARAH ELISABETH SAWYER EDITOR

ROCKHAVEN
PUBLISHING

Touch My Tears: Tales from the Trail of Tears

RockHaven Publishing
P.O. Box 1103
Canton, Texas 75103
SarahElisabethWrites.com/RockHavenPublishing

Edited by Sarah Elisabeth Sawyer

Interior Design: Sarah Elisabeth Sawyer

Cover Design: Josh McBride. josh360.com
Cover Image: Lynda Kay Sawyer

Illustrations: Leslie Widener and Beverly Bringle

Author Photo by R.A. Whiteside. Courtesy of the National Museum of the American Indian, Smithsonian Institution

Rising Fawn and the Fire Mystery by Marilou Awiakta © 2007 by Fulcrum Publishing. Reprinted with permission of the publisher
Okchakko: A Colt's Journey by Francine Locke Bray © 2013 by Francine Locke Bray. Printed with permission of the author
My Story—George Washington Choate by Jerry Colby © 2013 by Jerry Colby. Printed with permission of the author
Somewhere, William Wallace Smiled by James Masters © 2013 by James Masters. Printed with permission of the author
A Storm Blows the Family West by Curtis Pugh © 2013 by Curtis Pugh. Printed with permission of the author
Toward the Setting Sun by Ramona Choate Schrader © 2013 by Ramona Choate Schrader. Printed with permission of the author
Morning Came by Sarah Elisabeth Sawyer with Lynda Kay Sawyer © 2013 by Sarah Elisabeth Sawyer
Chi Pisa La Chike by Dianna Street © 2013 by Dianna Street. Printed with permission of the author
One Mississippi Clay Bowl by Leslie Widener © 2013 by Leslie Widener. Printed with permission of the author
Understand by Benjamin Zeller © 2013 by Benjamin Zeller. Printed with permission of the author

ISBN: 978-0-9910259-0-9
LCCN: 2013917940

This book is dedicated to our ancestors

who walked the trail for us.

Yakoke

CONTENTS

Foreword

As an olive-skinned woman with dark curly hair, I have been asked nearly every day of my life, "What are you?" My international friends assumed I am whatever they are: Greek, Italian, Latino, even Middle-Eastern. I was four years old the first time someone called me the *N-word*, and many of my African-American friends have supposed I'm at least part "black." When I was teaching English as a second language to a small group of Hispanic kindergartners, one of my students found a photo of my husband and fell to the floor in hysterical laughter. He shouted to the others, between giggles, "Mrs. Julie married a bald white man!" He had no idea I was not Hispanic.

Regardless of how others labeled me, my family has always identified ourselves as "white" even though many of my relatives tend to tan well like me.

I grew up in Louisiana, a place where our colorful culture is notoriously mixed. While people regularly have commented on my appearance, I have been completely comfortable with my skin color, the texture of my hair, and whatever identity people wanted to throw at me. But I also have been intrigued by the mysterious question, "What are you?"

Throughout my life, my family members have mentioned Choctaw and Scots-Irish roots, and after extensive genealogical research, I have discovered we have Cherokee ties as well. Still, I knew nothing about any of these cultures. Specifically, I knew no words of the Choctaw language, had never learned any of the traditional dances, and certainly never learned to weave swamp cane baskets, bead intricate designs, or embroider dresses for special ceremonies. I never cooked fry bread, played stickball, or attended a powwow. I never was given the privilege of identifying myself as Choctaw…and what a privilege that would have been.

When I reached my mid-thirties, I decided to write a novel. I had no idea what the story would be, but when I sat down to write, I was given the coming-of-age tale of a girl named Millie Reynolds. She was part Choctaw, living in Mississippi during the 1930s-40s, and she faced many obstacles in her life, including the tendency of the community to discard her as a lower-class citizen because of her Choctaw blood.

I never intended to write about the Choctaws, but the story was delivered to me unexpectedly—an experience some Choctaws believe was divine intervention, an ancestor relying on me to give voice to her important story. Whatever the explanation, I am grateful Millie shared her story with me, and I am even more grateful that the generous tribal community of the Mississippi Band of Choctaw Indians (MBCI), as well as many members of the Choctaw Nation of Oklahoma, have helped me to learn more about this missing piece of my heritage.

When asked what they want non-Choctaws to know, many Choctaws have provided a simple answer. As one tribal member put it, "We want people to know we're still here."

And what a testimony that is to the character and strength of the Choctaw people. Despite centuries of forced removal, aggressive brutality, fractured families, economic hardships, intentional betrayals, and destructive deceit, this tribe remains a vibrant and healthy community. Today, the Choctaws are the third largest federally-recognized tribe in the United States.

While I have always felt drawn to the Choctaw culture, and recent genealogical studies seem to have proven my Choctaw roots, I still feel uncomfortable calling myself Choctaw. I do not want to be disrespectful to the many Choctaws (and other Native Americans) who have maintained a direct connection to their tribal heritage. But, I admit, when Sarah Elisabeth shared her beautiful video about her work to preserve Choctaw Removal stories, I cried. What brought me to tears was not the wonderful research that Sarah Elisabeth is accomplishing with other Choctaw writers, although that has inspired me tremendously, it was the comment from Gary Batton, Assistant Chief of the Choctaw Nation of Oklahoma, who said: "Even if we have a Choctaw that's one/one-millionth, they need to understand, that's what makes them Choctaw."

It is understandable that many Choctaw tribal members tend to resent outsiders. It's all too common for a stranger to show up at the tribal office expecting to receive an "Indian card" because they claim to be some kind of Indian princess descended from an ancient chief whose name they do not know. But there are other Choctaws who understand the positive potential of helping those who are genuinely interested in understanding their roots.

I've since been told by some Choctaws that they welcome people like me, we "mixed-bloods" who are being nudged at some primal level to learn more about our origins. One MBCI member laughed and said that if anyone tells you he's full blood anything, he probably doesn't know what he's talking about (although this comment would surely incite anger among certain members of the tribe). She went on to say that she hopes every Choctaw, no matter how far removed, would take time to learn the true history of the tribe, to hear the stories of ancestors, and to help strengthen the Choctaw community.

Asst. Chief Batton added, "I disagree with the whole blood quantum issue only because I feel that this is just another way the government is trying to make us fight among ourselves. There is not another ethnic group (such as the Hispanics, African Americans, Irish, etc.) who has to prove their blood quantum. To me it is like saying you are only one-fourth American. In my opinion, either you are or you are not. It is more about your culture, your past, and your heart that makes you an American and those same things are what make you Choctaw."

Another tribal member had even more to say on the issue, adding: "We've been separated for too long, for reasons that were out of our control, but this—we can control. Now is our time to come back together."

And that's what the Choctaws have done for me. They have helped me answer, at least partly, the forty-year-old question, "What are you?"

Today, I am proud to say I am Choctaw. I am Scots-Irish. I am Cherokee.

I am Human. And I am here.

—**Julie Cantrell, author of *Into the Free***
and *When Mountains Move*

Introduction

Legacy Preservation

How do you preserve history, culture, and values for generations when there is no written language? Through story. Oral storytelling is an old tradition for Choctaws as it is with many cultures throughout the world. Our ancestors knew the lives they lived and the lessons they learned were important enough to pass on. They did this by telling stories regularly to their children and grandchildren, who in turn matured and passed those stories, as well as their own, to the next generation.

But a time came when these stories began to be forgotten. In boarding school, children were forbidden to tell them in their native language. They became the elders, and concealed the stories of their lives. It became shameful to be Choctaw.

However, in the midst of this loss, Choctaws still carried

tradition, language, and story into the next decade and the next. The tribe flourished and grew to the third largest in the United States. And our stories are still alive today.

How many stories have been lost, stories of everyday lives we could learn from? Countless. But there are those Choctaw writers who preserve the history. The work goes far beyond preservation.

We are sharing our stories with the world

Cultural expert Olin Williams says, "The world needs to know about our history. We need to get our stories down so we can tell others who we are."

We tell the stories. In our native language, in English, in writing. We tell of the Trail of Tears, the prejudices, the injustices. But we also tell of the triumphs and the faith.

Treaty of Dancing Rabbit Creek

This treaty was the single most important treaty made between the United States and the Choctaw Nation. It forced the Choctaw people to leave their Mississippi homelands for an unknown and, in their eyes, lesser territory.

It wasn't just about leaving or what monetary possessions they were losing. This was their home from ancient times.

They were connected to the land in a way the white man did not comprehend

The bones of their ancestors rested there. *Nanih Waiya,* the sacred mound, could not move with them.

How did such a treaty take place? Four major groups were instrumental in negotiating various treaties and agreements: the Choctaw Nation, the U.S. government, the Christian missionaries, and the settlers of the State of Mississippi. Greed served as the driving factor, hunger for land and westward expansion. Celebrations took place among Mississippians when Andrew Jackson was elected to the presidency. "Remove or be annihilated" became the running threat against the Choctaw people.

The U.S. government had forced treaties on the Choctaws for many years. And for as many years, the government had broken those same treaties, sometimes even before the ink dried on the signatures. In early treaties, Choctaws gave up millions of acres of land both in the Alabama and Mississippi territories. This was primarily to repay debts incurred at the government trading posts, set up for that purpose.

In September 1830, the fateful negotiations began at the meeting place of Dancing Rabbit Creek. Some say the main Choctaw leaders walked away near the end, refusing to sign the treaty, and other leaders stepped in to get what they could from the deal. Some say there was simply no choice if they wanted to preserve their status as a nation. Regardless the motivations, on September 27, 1830, the Treaty of Dancing Rabbit Creek was signed and the fate of the Choctaw Nation, sealed.

This forced a heartbreaking decision: go to the wilderness country west of Arkansas and remain a nation or stay behind among the white people in Mississippi. If they stayed, they were promised farmland and United States citizenship. But they would have to be neighbors with strangers, some of whom were thieves and murderers. The people were split as to whether they should go or stay. Lifelong friends divided. Clans divided. Families divided. But most came to the realization that giving up their homeland and going west was inevitable.

The Trail of Tears

The long journey began in 1831, spread over three main trips, all disastrous for the Choctaw Removal from Mississippi to Indian Territory (present day Oklahoma). One Choctaw chief is noted for saying to a reporter,

"This has been a trail of tears and death."

Thus originated the term *Trail of Tears*, used to this day to describe the removals of the five "civilized" tribes of the eastern United States.

During the Trail of Tears—which primarily took place over three years—an estimated two thousand of the twenty thousand Choctaws perished from disease, hunger, cold, and drowning. At age eleven, one of my great-grandfathers buried his father along the trail.

Despite the hardships and loss, the Choctaw Nation found ways to thrive in the new land. Their primary tool in this was establishing the tribe as a Christian nation. One section in the 1857 Constitution of the Choctaw Nation states: "No person who denies the being of a God, or a future state of rewards and punishments, shall hold any office in the civil department of this nation, nor shall he be allowed his oath in any court of justice."

Each year, our commemorative Trail of Tears walk is opened with prayer. We remember those who walked the trail for us. We remember the Creator who brought us through.

The Treaty of Dancing Rabbit Creek was a catalyst to horrific and unjust events. But placed in God's hands, it was a step toward where the Choctaw Nation of Oklahoma is today.

Oklahoma is another story to be told. It shows how two cultures have accepted each other and grown together into a great state. "Oklahoma" is a Choctaw word meaning Red People.

The Challenge of this Collection

The tragedies and triumphs of this marked event in both U.S. and Choctaw history inspired the challenging undertaking of compiling this anthology of Removal stories. Some are based on family stories. Some are based on general historical facts.

They all draw on the spirit of the Choctaw people
to overcome, to persevere, to thrive

This is celebrated throughout the collection, while not forgetting the One who did not leave nor forsake our nation.

Choctaw authors from five states spent months meticulously researching and capturing the facts as well as the emotions of our ancestors and the journey they endured. Not all walked the same trail nor during the same time periods. Following the main three trips, the Removal went on for decades with small bands deciding they would join those already in Indian Territory.

Our stories are in danger of not only being lost forever with the forgotten memories of our elders, but are in danger of obscurity in online and federal archives. Our mission is to preserve these in a way that not only insures our children and grandchildren can someday read them, but that they reach audiences around the world.

The stories you are about to read are not in chronological order. Rather, they are arranged to give you background and details, building on each other as you experience the Trail of Tears. Most of the characters in the stories speak Choctaw; however, the dialogue is shown in English with a taste of Choctaw words added in. You will find a glossary of Choctaw words located at the back of the book.

The Choctaw Nation of Oklahoma represents the resilience and faith of a people to overcome in spite of their tragedies. And their many tears.

Touch them through our stories.

Chahta siah hoke,
I am Choctaw,
Sarah Elisabeth Sawyer

ChoctawSpirit.com

You number my wanderings;

Put my tears into Your bottle;

Are they not in Your book?

Psalm 56:8 (NKJV)

RISING FAWN AND THE
FIRE MYSTERY

Marilou Awiakta with Beverly Bringle

In December 1982, Irving Knight said, "I want to tell you about my great-grandmother…" That was the beginning of this story, which Mr. Knight gave Marilou Awiakta permission to tell. The rest of its Choctaw context fell into place later when Beverly Bringle showed Marilou the account of her great-grandfather Tushpa, written by his son, James Culberson.

"Beverly and I resolved to try to create a story that would be like an Indian flute, an instrument that voices from the past could sing through to reach people of all ages today. From that moment on, we worked with one mind…"—Awiakta.

Acknowledged as a classic in Native American literature, *Rising Fawn and the Fire Mystery* has received formal recognition in a variety of ways, from stage plays to the Auckland, New Zealand, school system. Heritage, family, and courage enabled Rising Fawn to survive, and for more than three decades her story has quietly made its way into the hearts of people both in America and abroad.

"A story that's meant to be told comes in the fullness of its own time and in its own way."—Awiakta.

Rising Fawn and the
Fire Mystery

Marilou Awiakta with Beverly Bringle

"Grandmother, will we have to leave our home?"

"Your father comes back from the Council to-night, Rising Fawn. He will tell us."

It was the fourth night of the Cold Moon, the winter of Rising Fawn's seventh year. Her family had drawn their chairs around the cabin hearth, for chill air seeped through cracks in the shutters and narrow spaces between the floor planks.

Rising Fawn huddled on the Grandmother's lap. She took comfort in the familiar scent of the old woman, a clean, earthy scent mixed with the faint tang of warm pine. With that stout bosom at her back and the Grandmother's hands clasped across her chest like a clump of gnarled roots, Rising Fawn felt safe. She liked to feel the hands. Beneath their wrinkled, brown skin, the flesh was still firm and strong close to the bone.

Ishtoua, the Grandmother. Ishtoua, the deliverer. Her wisdom would protect the family. And yet, she had not said they would be safe. Rising Fawn was afraid.

Her mother put aside the shirt she was sewing and got up to stir the fire, making the flames leap and crackle. Then she laid her hand on the wood chimney and ran her fingers along the grooves in the clay chinking.

"Your father's fingers made these grooves. When we married, the clan helped hew the logs and raise the cabin. But he smoothed every chink…"

Rising Fawn's brother, Kowichosh, had stopped reading his book and was studying his mother's face. Kowichosh, the bobcat. Quick-sighted. Quick-tempered. He was only twice Rising Fawn's age, but his face was already setting in the lines of a young warrior.

"They should not be allowed to take our land," he said. "They want it for more cotton fields, more money. In the three years since the Treaty of Dancing Rabbit Creek, they've taken almost everything that belonged to the Choctaw!"

His mother returned to her chair and took up the shirt, pushing the needle in and out of the blue wool she had carded, spun, and dyed herself. The daughter of Ishtoua was not easily pushed to anger or despair. "I can't believe our white neighbors would betray us. We speak their language. Our children play together. The chiefs and elders have listened to their missionaries with respect."

"Mother, over six thousand Choctaw have already been removed. Hundreds have died on the march West. Why should the Government let us stay?"

"Perhaps they won't, Kowichosh." His mother paused in the middle of a stitch and looked at him firmly. "You are a good scholar at school. You understand many things. But you do not understand this…We can't give up hope until we know we must leave everything behind."

Abashed, Kowichosh turned back to his book, but Rising Fawn mulled the words, "leave everything behind...!" Leave school and friends...woods...fields of corn...the rock-rimmed pool in the creek where the family bathed every day, summer and winter...the cabin with its smell of wood fire, the crisp scent of drying meat and summer vegetables hanging from the rafters...the loft where she slept with the Grandmother on a mattress stuffed with corn shucks and pine boughs...

How the Grandmother loved pine! In the family cemetery, with its small wooden house over each grave, she had chosen a plot for herself beneath a large pine. Twice a year, the family gathered for the cry ceremony to assure the spirits of the dead that their bones were cared for. And the Grandmother often said to Rising Fawn, "One day, you will join the cry of the kindred for me. My spirit will hover near. I will be happy, as our ancestors have been when we remember them."

Rising Fawn nestled against the Grandmother. If they left everything behind, who would care for the bones of the family? Who would comfort their spirits? If the Grandmother should die, there would be no one left to remember. Rising Fawn wished her father would come. But the fire had burned low before they heard footsteps and the sound of the latch-string. Everyone looked toward the door. Bending his head to miss the top of the doorjamb, her father came quietly into the room. Snow powdered his buckskin jacket and clung to strands of his hair. As he greeted them, his face was weary and sad. He put another log on the fire, warmed his hands before the new flames, then, standing with his back to the hearth, he spoke slowly.

"The Council has debated for many days. Our clan chiefs and elders have decided—any of us who stay in Mississippi are a marked people. Already, soldiers have burned some of our cabins to force us out. We must go to Indian Territory. We must leave our home."

The words passed through the family with the tremor of an earthquake and the ground beneath them seemed to shake and crack. They felt themselves falling into a bottomless dark.

For a time, there was no sound except the steady sigh of the fire.

Rising Fawn clung to the Grandmother's hands. Kowichosh sat stiff and defiant. The Grandmother gazed steadily into the flames.

"How can we go?" asked the mother. "Our clan has many children and elders. The Big River is high and the current runs swift, carrying many logs and branches. What does the Chief Headman say?"

"Chief Baha says our band will number almost a hundred. We will wait until the river goes down before we leave. Below Friar's Point, where Mulberry Island breaks the stream, the current is less swift. He has crossed safely there many times. The Government will not keep its promise to send boats and wagons, so we will have to build rafts and canoes. During the Moon of Wind, we will cross. After that, we will walk."

"How long is the journey?"

"Four hundred miles."

Silence again. No one looked at the Grandmother. Such a distance was beyond her strength. She would surely die along the trail.

"Why don't our white neighbors help us?" Kowichosh asked. "The Choctaw have lived with them in peace. Our warriors fought with General Jackson against the British. Where are our white friends now?"

"They tell us they are sorry," the father said, "but it is the

Government's doing and they cannot help us."

Kowichosh clenched his fists. "Then we should fight!"

"No. Long ago, our chiefs and headmen gave their spoken word that the Choctaw would kill no white man of this country. For any of us to break that word would be a disgrace. Your blood is hot. You have no wisdom."

In a voice like bare branches rubbing in the wind, the Grandmother spoke. "When white people first came to our country, we were many and they were few. They needed us. Now we are few and they are many. They want our land. If we fight, there will be death on both sides, and in the end, we will still have to go."

Shaking his head, Kowichosh started to protest, but the Grandmother raised her hand. "The Choctaw must keep a moving spirit within us. Our spirit is our sacred fire. All your life, Grandson, you have seen how the sacred fire is kept burning in the Council House. Its flames are one with the sun and the Giver of Life. In the fall, during Loak Mosholi, the fire is put on the ceremonial grounds. You have seen how we bring a brand from it to rekindle our hearths. Is the meaning of this lost to you? If you want to be a true warrior, give your strength to the spirit of your people."

When the rest of the family had gone to bed, the Grandmother moved the chairs and spread her blanket in the old way before the hearthstones. With another blanket wrapped around her, she sat facing the embers.

From her place in the loft, Rising Fawn looked down and the tremors within her quieted.

The Grandmother was praying for her people.

As the Cold Moon waxed larger, many of the Twin Lakes Clan came to the cabin—grandmothers, grandfathers, aunts, and uncles. They spoke of sorrow and fear, of how to help each other. Most of all, they came to touch the wisdom of the Grandmother, who was the eldest.

Watching the family gather strength, Rising Fawn grew hopeful. But she went even more quietly than usual about her chores. Her mother smiled and said, "You are a child of your name—silent and quick. And those calm deer eyes miss nothing—you and your Grandmother are alike in that. You two should choose the seed corn."

On one end of the worn plank table, she heaped shucked ears. Some were deep orange. Others had gold kernels mingled with russet and soft black. "The chiefs and elders have given everyone a task for the journey and for making a home in the new land. We are to take choice seed corn for the fields. Your father and brother have brought deerskins for pouches. The fur will shed water and keep the seeds dry."

"And we must have seed enough for a large field," said the Grandmother. "The corn is like our people; it draws strength from its clan. A single stalk will bear nothing." How well the Grandmother knew the ways of corn. As she twisted an ear in her hands, kernels pattered onto the table so fast that Rising Fawn was kept busy scooping them into a willow basket. When it was full, she poured the kernels onto the table. They began to cull those too dark and hard to sprout.

From a pile of skins beside the fireplace, the mother took one, laid it on the floor, and knelt to measure it. Rising Fawn peered over the edge of the table. "I want to carry seeds too. Will you make me a pouch?"

"I will make one small, like you, and put it on a thong so you can wear it around your neck. You must not lose it. It is a sacred task to carry seeds for the people, for if the seeds are lost, the people will go hungry."

Rising Fawn was pleased and her curiosity quickened about

the new land. "In the West, Grandmother, will there be a new sky? Will there be a Cup of Stars in the sky like we have here to tell us when to plant the corn?"

Her question made the Grandmother chuckle. "Of course, little one. Only land changes. The sky will be the same. When the Cup of Stars turns upside down like a dipper spilling water, we will know that Mother Earth is ready to receive the seed. The Great Spirit has made all things in harmony and the wisdom of the Great Spirit is within each thing."

She pressed a round russet kernel into Rising Fawn's palm.

"Its heart is like a tiny flame of sacred fire. But feel how tough the shell is. You can throw the seed on the floor, put it in a pouch, carry it in your hand, but it will sprout only in warm earth. If it spouts too soon, it will die. It protects itself until it is safe—that is its wisdom. The seed lives deep in its spirit until the time to come forth."

Closing Rising Fawn's hand around the kernel, she held the small fist in her root-like fingers. "The journey to the West will be hard. You will have to endure much. Be like the seed. Protect yourself. Live deep in your spirit until the time to come forth."

Rising Fawn turned this thought in her mind, then she asked, "How will I know when the time has come?"

"Listen to the wisdom within, where the Great Spirit speaks to you."

"Grandmother, when you pray before the fire, are you listening?"

"The fire is a relative of the sun and of the Life Giver. It helps me listen for the Great Spirit. When I pray, I am listening...with my spirit-eyes and my spirit-ears."

Rising Fawn looked at the fire. "I see flames. I hear them snap and roar. That is all."

"You are using your body-eyes and body-ears," said the Grandmother. With her fingers, she tapped Rising Fawn's chest. "You must listen with your spirit-eyes and spirit-ears."

"Can you teach me how to listen?"

The Grandmother shook her head. "All I can teach you is to be still. You must ponder the fire mystery for yourself."

That night, Rising Fawn tried hard to be still and pray with the Grandmother. She kept her eyes on the fire, but her mind circled the room. It touched the heavy deerskin pouches piled by the door…the loft where her brother was sleeping…the corner bed where her parents slept…the gourds filled with sugar and meal…the spinning wheel, her father's gun…baskets of berries, beans and squash…firelight dancing on her beaded moccasins…the snakeskin design glistening on her red dress… the small pouch, plump with seeds, around her neck…the Granmother's eyes.

The eyes of the Grandmother were smiling, a smile that seemed to say, "To ponder a mystery takes patience. You are young. There is time."

Long after the Grandmother had gone to her bed in the loft, Rising Fawn lay on the blanket and gazed into the fire. She was warm and drifting to sleep when she felt a darkness gather about her, a faint tremor in the boards beneath her. Her first dazed thought was "Earthquake!" Then she realized horses were galloping close to the cabin. A shout brought her wide awake, a white man's shout…

"Burn it down! Gimme that torch. I'll throw it!"

Above the sound of hooves, another taut, urgent shout, "At least wake the family first, for god's sake!"

For answer, there was a thud against the cabin wall.

"Soldiers!" cried the father. He leapt from bed and climbed the loft ladder. "Wake up! Wake up!" Suddenly everyone else was moving—grabbing blankets, clothes, and as many pouches as they could carry. Rising Fawn stood by the hearth, holding her blanket around her. Through the cracks between the logs of the walls, smoke seeped into the room and she heard the warning of the flames.

Her mother thrust a heavy pouch into her hands. "Quick! Unbolt the door!"

She slid back the bolt, darted among the skittish horses. Startled, one horse reared above her. An arm jerked her out of the way; her dress sleeve tore...the large pouch dropped. Hooves crashed down on it, seed corn scattered across the muddy snow. At the same time, she felt herself being drawn onto a saddle and held tightly against a rough coat that smelled of smoke and damp wool. She struggled and cried out, but the grim-faced soldier muttered, "At least I'll save one."

Beneath the pounding feet of the horse, the earth seemed once more to shake and crack. The crescent moon swung back and forth in the sky. Rising Fawn felt herself falling into a darkness that became a dream. Her arms grew heavy, her eyelids heavier. She woke once in a half daze.

After a time, the pounding hooves gave way to a powerful rocking and a sound of churning water. She dreamed the Big River flowed cold around her. A cottonwood tree torn from its bank somewhere upriver swung heavily at her. She fought the wet branches—her fingers tore at the bark. She seemed caught in an endless cycle—rocking, rocking. She pulled her blanket around her and pressed the deerskin pouch against her cheek. She tasted the salt of her tears.

In the sky, the Grandmother's hand tilted the Cup of Stars

toward the earth. A voice like the embrace of wind in the pines whispered, "Be like the seed...live deep in your spirit..."

All motion stopped.

Rising Fawn opened her eyes.

She was in a box! Air and sunlight filtered through a crack in the lid, and she saw long scratches in the wood where she had tried to get out. Her fingers were raw and sore.

She heard a knocking...

A white man's voice shouted, "Christmas gift!"

A bolt sliding back. A door opening.

"Michael!" a woman cried. "Come quick, James."

Another man's voice, this time heartier and older. "Welcome home, Michael. You're early. We didn't expect you in Memphis 'til Christmas Eve. Here, let me help you with that box." Rising Fawn felt a lifting, a carrying, a setting down. "I see you've marked it 'Clothes,' Michael. Mighty heavy for just clothes."

"It isn't clothes," said the soldier. "It's something much more valuable. Something you and Amanda have wanted for a very long time..."

Light thumps of rope untying. Then the lid slowly sliding off.

In the bright light, the white faces blurred above her and Rising Fawn saw clearly only a grizzled beard, a yellow mustache, and a coil of yellow braided hair. She clutched her deerskin pouch and felt tough kernels press against her palm. *"Be like the seed...Be like the seed."*

The woman bent closer. "It's a child, James—an Indian child!"

"Well, now…" The man with the grizzled beard laid his callused hand on Rising Fawn's. Then he lifted her in his arms and went to sit in a chair beside the hearth.

Rising Fawn glanced furtively about the room—wood chimney, log walls, plank table, square bed in the corner. The cabin could be her own home—except that the people were white, and strangers. Like a young doe trying to escape notice, she became very still. For a few moments, the strangers were still also. Rising Fawn heard their soft breathing, the steady whisper of the fire…the flutter and cluck of chickens nesting under the floor.

From the box the woman brought the blanket and tucked it around the child. Kneeling beside the chair, she smoothed Rising Fawn's hair and touched her cheek. "She has beautiful eyes…so brown you can't see to the bottom." She looked at the torn dress, the fingers raw with scratches. "How did you come by this child, Michael?"

"Last night, some men in my company got drunk and set on meanness. They knew about a Choctaw cabin in the woods near Friar's Point. They got it in their heads to burn it down. I tried to stop them. When I couldn't, I rode along to try to warn the family. I couldn't do that either. Things like this—and worse—happen all the time, Amanda. This removal is cruel work. I'm sick of it. When I saw that little girl run out of the burning cabin, something in me snapped. I grabbed her up and cut out…caught a steamboat at Friar's Point."

"What about her family?"

"Dead, maybe. If not, the cold will get them…or they'll die on the long walk West. I just said to myself, 'At least I'll save one.' And I did. Then I thought of you and James…'Course, some folks hereabouts might say bad of you for taking an Indian girl for your own…If you don't want her, I guess I could..."

Rising Fawn looked up at the man holding her. His eyes were warm and brown. "Hmf," he said. "Somebody's always saying bad about something. If you're quality folks—or poor like us—nobody cares much what you do. Besides, after all these years clerking at Winchester's store, I've traded with an abundance of Chickasaws and Choctaws. I figure in the main, they're peaceable people—and honest. We'll love this little one and raise her for our own, won't we, Amanda? Now you can use that trundle bed you've been saving all this time."

The woman went to her brother and took both his hands. "The child will be a blessing to us. But you've brought trouble on yourself—you've deserted the Army, haven't you?"

The brother nodded. "I have. So I'm headed West. A man can disappear out there and get a new start."

"When will you go?"

"Right away. The Army is probably already on my trail, but they'll be asking about a soldier with an Indian child. Nobody saw me with her, because of the box. Your place may be where they'll look for me next. On the way from the Landing, I stopped by Anderson's Hotel. Found some folks passing through on their way to Texas. I'm going with them on the next ferry."

The woman put her arms around him. "You're the only one of my family left, Michael. I can't bear to think of you so far away...especially at Christmas...among strangers."

"Don't fret about me, Amanda. Think of that little girl. You and James are all she has now."

Rising Fawn felt the three of them looking at her, but she fixed her eyes on the fire. The room, the faces, the things she had heard swirled in her mind and flowed away, except for the words *What about her family? Dead, maybe.* In the curling flames, she saw the currents of the Big River and she knew, for her father had taught her, that in water, all trails are lost. There was no way back to her family. No way for them to follow her, if any were alive to try.

Rising Fawn did not cry or speak. Her silence became a tough shell as she withdrew deep in her spirit...to be like the seed and wait for the time to come forth...to listen for the Great Spirit...

From then on, only the fire was real to her. She thought of the white couple as simply "the Man" and "the Woman." With her body-ears and body-eyes, she understood what they said, and she did as they asked, for they were Elders. But she never talked to them.

She turned her spirit to the fire. In the mornings, she watched the Woman unbank the embers and stir them to life, then she helped the Man carry out ashes. When he brought in logs, she walked beside him, her arms heaped with branches and strips of bark, which she later fed, one by one, to the flames.

During the day, there were many chores to do—making butter and cottage cheese, spinning, weaving, plain sewing, beans to shell, meat to cook—but as she worked with the Woman, Rising Fawn listened to the fire sing and crackle and sigh. She smelled the burning wood as it changed to warmth and light. At night, she sat on her blanket before the sandstone hearth, following the mysterious shift and leap of the flames. If she was very still, the spirit of the Grandmother came to sit beside her. But when Rising Fawn asked, "Are you well? Is my family well?" the Grandmother would not reply. The Great Spirit, too, was silent. And Rising Fawn knew she had not yet learned to be still enough.

"The child is *here*, but she isn't *with* us," the Woman told her

17

husband. "I wonder if she'll ever truly be our own."

"She's likely grieving for her own people, Amanda. We'd best leave her be. We've got to be patient and gentle her slow." They began by forbidding her to bathe every day. "It'll weaken you," they said. "Once every week or two is enough." The smell of their bodies and of her own was much too ripe. But Rising Fawn paid it no mind.

The Woman made a dress for her. Using the torn red one for a pattern, she cut gray woolsey and sewed the seams by hand. No beads. No snakeskin design. Rising Fawn wore the dress, but she paid it no mind.

She was proud of her black hair, worn loose and shining in the way of the grandmothers. But while the Woman plaited it in two long braids, Rising Fawn stood without flinching. She paid them no mind.

The Man bought her a pair of high-topped shoes that laced up the front. The stiff leather hurt her ankles and the soles were so thick that when she went to the woodpile or to the spring, Rising Fawn couldn't feel the softness of Mother Earth beneath her feet, like she did in moccasins. She wore the shoes, but she paid them no mind.

"One last thing," said the Woman, "and you will almost look like one of us." She grasped the deerskin pouch to take it off. Rising Fawn took her hand and gently pulled it away.

Stepping back, the Woman looked at her a long time, then shook her head sadly. Rising Fawn went to sit before the fire. She murmured to herself in Choctaw, "It is hard to be like the seed…"

Later, when she thought Rising Fawn was asleep, the Woman said in a low voice, "The child understands what we say, James. I'm sure she could speak, if she would. There's a knowing in her eye—and something else. Sometimes they seem like the eyes of an old woman, wise and distant. I think she has a pagan soul."

"Amanda, maybe it's just the difference you're seeing. You're used to white children."

"No. No. From the day she came, I've been watching her. She prays to the fire, worships it. I know that pouch is a heathen thing. Tomorrow we must take her to church. With Christmas so near, I'm sure Brother Owen will tell the story of the Christ Child. It will do her soul good to hear it."

The Man sighed. "Hearing is one thing. Accepting is another. Indians call God the Great Spirit, and they have different ways of worshiping him. You can change an Indian on the outside, but deep down, he'll keep to his own ways."

"That may be. But it can't do anybody harm to be in God's House."

Rising Fawn was listening. *Pagan* and *heathen* were unknown words to her, but they had a bad sound. She put them from her mind and puzzled over the other words that sounded good—*Christmas, Christ Child, God's House.* Sometimes she'd heard white children use the words, but Rising Fawn had never before been curious about what they meant. Maybe God's House was like the Choctaws' Council House. Maybe she would feel at home there.

The next morning, the Woman pinned a white collar on her black poplin dress and tucked the pouch under the bodice of Rising Fawn's gray one. "We don't wear ornaments in God's House," she said. "It's irreverent. You shouldn't wear that heathen pouch at all."

Inwardly, Rising Fawn smiled, because the pouch made a funny gray bump on her chest. "White people are strange," she thought. "Christmas must be one of their great ceremonies, with prayers and sacred dances and a feast. But they don't prepare for it. No bright clothes. No bead and feather symbols. Nothing to celebrate and honor the Great Spirit. Surely, though, they will have a sacred fire in their Council House..."

She looked forward to hearing about the Christ Child. When the clan elders told an important story, the Grand-mother always said, "In the telling is a wisdom for the people." And Rising Fawn was glad the Christmas story was about a child, like herself.

These things flickered in her mind as they set out in the wagon. She sat in the back, jostling with each lurch and bump. "It's a good thing we have clear skies," the Man said. "Rain in Memphis means mud to your knees and some of these holes are deep enough to drown an ox."

Rising Fawn was thinking of the thick woods on either side of the road. Branches swayed and rubbed together in the wind, like the voice of the Grandmother, speaking without words. The sound quieted her spirit and made her more aware of what was happening around her.

They turned into a wider road, with stumps newly cut, just low enough to let the wagon axle pass. Once in a while, the wheels would slip in a rut and bang the wagon bed on a stump. A bell was clanging in the distance.

"This is Poplar Street," the Man said over his shoulder. "Yonder in the field on Second—that little white frame building—that's the Methodist Meeting House. We built it last year. It's the only church in Memphis. Started with eleven members and now we have about fifty."

"And we have our own bell too," the Woman added. "It's

up on a pole and the preacher shakes the pole to ring it. Before that, we had to use the hotel bell to call the people." They sounded pleased and proud. As the wagon pulled up among high weeds in the churchyard, Rising Fawn saw many people gathering. Some came on foot. Some came on horseback. God's House surprised her. It was four-cornered, like the Council House, but instead of one door in front, there were two. Women were going in by the left door, men by the right. Inside, it was quiet and smelled of new wood. The walls were smooth and white. Sunlight streamed brightly through the clear glass windows. There was one aisle between two rows of benches made of planks laid loose on blocks, some high, some low.

Rising Fawn sat with the Woman on the left side. She wondered why everyone faced forward. Without a circle, how would the chiefs and elders see each other when they spoke? And why did the people wear such drab, dull colors? Rising Fawn was glad to see many dark faces among the white. Some were black and shining, like sun on a raven's wing. Others were warm brown shades of Mother Earth. Beside her, a slim woman with skin almost like her own smiled at her. Rising Fawn smiled back.

But she was disturbed. Nowhere was there a sacred fire. And the ceremony seemed odd. Someone struck a tuning fork and the people sang. Rising Fawn caught one phrase, "how sweet the sound..." The sound was sweet, but there was no drum, no steady dancing beat. Perhaps the dances would come later.

Oddest of all, when the people prayed, they bowed their heads and closed their eyes. How could they hear the Great Spirit if they turned their faces away, if they didn't listen with their eyes as well as their ears?

After the prayer, the Woman whispered, "Brother Owen will preach now. You'll like him. Sometimes he soars aloft and takes us into the third heaven."

Rising Fawn made no sense of these words, except that Brother Owen must be a chief who had the power of an eagle. Quietly, he began the story of the Christ Child and the great star that foretold his birth. At the word *star*, Rising Fawn leaned forward to listen better.

Then the Chief began to speak of a "king mighty in his wickedness" and of "Light overcoming Darkness." He uttered strange words like *sin* and *redemption*. Rising Fawn lost the thread of the story. She began to listen, not to the words, but to their rhythm, which rose and fell and rose again. The Chief did not pause for any elders to speak, but went on and on. As he talked, he waved his arms. The waving became faster as his voice rose louder and higher—up, up, up. Rising Fawn expected him to mount into the air.

Instead, a bench gave way and five people fell to the floor.

There was more singing. Brother Owen raised his hand for a prayer. And the ceremony was over.

Outside again, people seemed satisfied and happy. They greeted each other and some called out "Merry Christmas" as they parted.

Bumping along the road in the wagon, Rising Fawn was glad when the churchyard ended and the trees began again. She listened to the wind flow from tree to tree, moving along beside her, and she whispered in Choctaw, "Grandmother... these people are strange beyond all knowing. Their spirit has no sacred fire. Their ceremony has no dance. And they leave the Christ Child with his story half-told. How can anyone learn its wisdom if the story is half-told?"

The stirring of the branches reminded her, *"Be like the seed.*

Live deep in your spirit...Be still, listen..." But when the wagon crossed a street edged with log houses, Rising Fawn entered a boisterous world that sent her spirit skittering like corn across a stone floor.

"Market Square—the center of town," announced the Man. He stopped the wagon by a hard-packed plot dotted with tall trees. Around the square were low buildings, made of boards or hewn logs. The Man pointed out several stores, the court-house, and the jail, saying, "They bring the prisoners across the street there to Anderson's Hotel for meals. Guess they figure a hungry man won't bolt! Next to the jail is..."

But Rising Fawn was too startled to pay attention. Hogs were rooting in heaps of garbage that had been thrown into the street. The door of one of the cabins opened and a woman emptied a chamber pot near the doorstep. The Grandmother always said, "No self-respecting animal—or person—fouls its own nest." But the smell and look of the square was certainly foul!

Two women were walking across the square. One wore a fire-red dress and a hat with red and pink feathers. The other was dressed all in purple. Although their faces were painted and their clothes bright, Rising Fawn was sure they were not headed for a ceremony. Perhaps it was because of the way they stopped to laugh and talk with the men. Most of the people in the square were men. Some wore buckskins and were riding horses—most likely trappers. Others stomped along in boots and denims, talking loudly and making jokes.

A mule pulling a small farm wagon stepped in a deep hole in the road and could not get out. No matter how hard the farmer swore and pulled on the bridle, the mule could not be budged. The farmer unhitched the wagon, pulled it off to the side of the road, and went into a saloon, leaving the mule to save himself.

The Woman shook her head and said to Rising Fawn, "Now you see why respectable womenfolk never come to town alone. Between flatboatmen, Indians, and, yes, men from hereabouts drinking and acting like heathens, the streets aren't safe."

"Don't forget the bears, Amanda," the Man said wryly. "Sometimes they wander in from the woods, not to mention the panthers and polecats."

"Hmf! I'd rather face any one of them than some of these men. What Mayor Rawlings ought to do is close down the saloons and build more churches. Whiskey leads to dancing, you know."

"Amanda, you're forgetting that the Methodists used to meet in the Blue Ruin Tavern before they built the church."

"We just met in the dining room, not the bar," she answered sharply.

To Rising Fawn, the connections the Woman made between dancing, heathens, whiskey, and church were confusing. The elders had always been stern about whiskey. It was forbidden. That much, at least, she understood. The men she saw made her nervous because most of them were bearded, and Choctaw men never were. Oddly, apart from the first moment she saw him, she had never been frightened of the Woman's husband. In fact, she hardly noticed his beard anymore. Perhaps it was because he was so kindly.

As he clucked to the horse and the wagon moved around the corner to Main Street, he said over his shoulder, "Guess all this noise is a little upsetting to you, child. But Memphis is just now sprouting into a town. We're getting civilized. We have a newspaper called the *Advocate*, and a town council. Sometimes Sol Smith brings his players down from Cincinnati. We'll have to take you to see Mr. and Mrs. Marks in 'The Day After the Fair,' or 'The Lover's Quarrel.' I expect we can get Sister Ann Kesterson to come from the church to teach you your letters. If you were a boy—and we had some money or some land to trade for the teaching—you could go to the Irishman, Mr. Magevney. He keeps school in a cabin near our place. There's plans to make a square there too—'Court Square,' I think they call it. So far, the square's no more than a few stakes in the woods, but it'll get cleared by and by."

Rising Fawn was only half listening. Among the stores and houses on Main Street were many trees and she watched them as much as she could, trying to keep in touch with the voice of the Grandmother. But when the wagon turned into a narrow alley, she saw only a few scraggly bushes, some old papers, meat bones, a soggy feather mattress, and a dead dog among the buildings.

"Now this shackledy place," said the Man, stopping the wagon, "is all that's left of the Bell Tavern—just enough left standing for a bar. Last winter, some poor folks got mighty cold. Ol' Judge Overton over in Nashville owns a lot of forest property around here, but he wouldn't let a soul get any firewood from it. So some folks came and chopped up all the Tavern's sleeping rooms for firewood. Then hogs got into it, rooting and knocking the boards loose, and that's all that's left."

It sounded as if the hogs were still in it. Rising Fawn heard grunts, shouts, thumps, and shattering glass. Pulling the wagon to the side of the alley, the Man said, "A big fight's going on in there. Wait a bit and you'll see a sight. Hear that clatter and shouting off in the distance? They're bringing up our fire engine, Little Vigor."

Eight men soon came running down the alley, pulling a

bell-shaped pump about three feet high. Other men, curious and eager, ran alongside.

The Woman looked alarmed. "Move on, James. They're liable to get in a big way and douse us too!"

"Now, Amanda, we don't want to miss the fun. We'll be all right."

When the engine was in place, six men began to pump the cranks. While one man held open the Tavern door, another aimed the hose at the opening. Such a foul-smelling stream of water rushed out that Rising Fawn held her nose.

The Man chuckled. "They've filled her up again at the hog wallow down at Auction Square." Suddenly, men burst out of the tavern, swearing, staggering, holding their arms in front of their faces as they ran in all directions.

The wagon moved on too. "Yes, sir, be it a fight or a fire, Little Vigor can take care of it. She can throw a stream over the highest house in town, which I'm going to show to you directly. It's right around here where Chickasaw runs into Mississippi Row. By the way, there's the Blue Ruin. They call it that because they say when folks drink a lot of gin there, it turns their skin blue!"

The building was painted bright blue too. Rising Fawn liked the color, but the Woman said, "James, you do beat all. What's the child going to think of us!"

Soon they came to a two-story frame house, set in a grove of bare-limbed locust trees. Slowing the wagon, the Man said, "This is Major Winchester's—and that's his store there beside it, where I work."

Raccoon and deer hides were tacked to the wall and goods lined the porch of the store—sacks of corn, piles of skins, a heavy bedstead, a plow—and there was a sign nailed to a post that, the Man told Rising Fawn, said, "Clothes—Blue, Black, and Fancy." A tall Indian was examining the bedstead. From his belted chintz tunic and the turban on his head, Rising Fawn knew he was Chickasaw. She felt a sharp loneliness for her own people and a yearning to be at home again. "Major Winchester," the Man went on, "is one of the quality folks in Memphis. Was our first mayor. Now he's the Postmaster and Land Agent. This is the only two-story house in Memphis... even has a ballroom on the second floor."

The Woman frowned. "Dancing leads to all manner of wickedness! That's why Josiah Baker was thrown out of church last year. Somebody caught him looking in the hotel ballroom and tapping his foot. Dancing is a heathen practice. No child of mine will ever have any part of it."

Brisk and impatient, the wind rattled the branches of the locust trees and Rising Fawn murmured, "Did you hear what she said, Grandmother? 'Dancing leads to wickedness.' How can sacred dancing be wicked? I will never understand these people. I don't want to be in their noisy, confusing world."

As the wagon rolled along the promenade, Rising Fawn looked out over the Bluff. Beyond the expanse of tall grass and blackberry brambles, the Big River stretched wide and swift—the great, muddy waters where all trails are lost. Memories of the burning cabin and the night of endless rocking flowed around her. She began to shake and her heart cried out, "Grandmother...Grandmother..."

Having no trees to give it voice, the Grandmother's spirit swept away down the river.

Rising Fawn lay down on her side in the wagon bed, with her legs drawn up, curling her head to her knees. When she heard the Woman ask what was the matter, she did not even look up. And when they were at the cabin again, Rising Fawn withdrew even deeper into her kernel of silence.

That night, the spirit of the Grandmother did not come to sit by the hearth. Nor did she come the next night, or the next. To Rising Fawn, the mystery of the fire was hidden more than ever. Why had the Grandmother left her alone? Why did the Great Spirit not speak? Would there ever be a time to come forth or would the flame of her spirit go out and leave her useless, like a culled seed? The wondering was so great that she became more and more still. And the Man and Woman rarely talked, even to each other.

Because there were no words to distract her, Rising Fawn began to listen with her spirit-eyes and spirit-ears. Gradually, she began to see the fire not only as a cherished link with home and family, but as a living presence with a spirit of its own. Sitting within the circle of its warm and shifting light, she felt the tough, thick shell around her soften and grow more thin.

For the first time, she noticed that the Woman's eyes were hazel and sad with yearning. She remembered her bending over a gray woolsey, sewing seams with careful stitches, remembered her saying to the Man, "I wonder if the child will ever truly be our own?"

And the Man had said, "She's likely grieving for her own people. Leave her be." He understood so much. And he had been the first to say, "We'll love her and raise her for our own." Now he seemed distant and his step was slower, older.

Rising Fawn sensed the Man and Woman were thinking about her too. Out of the corners of her eyes, she often saw them watch her, then look a long time at each other. Once the Woman bowed her head, as if to hide tears, and the Man touched her gently on the cheek.

Rising Fawn had never realized before how alone they were. No one from their clan ever came to comfort and cheer them. She had listened to them only with her body-eyes and body-ears. And it was not enough.

The Grandmother had once said, "All I can teach you is to be still."

Rising Fawn murmured, "I have learned, Grandmother. You have taught me by your coming—and by your going—how to be still. Come back and show me the mystery of the fire…"

One morning, when the sun was high, Rising Fawn woke to a new stir in the cabin and the smell of frying sidemeat. The Woman was at the hearth tending iron pots that sat among the coals or hung on hooks above the fire. Over her homespun dress, she wore a fresh white apron, and over her hair, a muslin cap that tied under her chin.

Rising Fawn heard her say, "Get up, child, and rejoice. It's Christmas! The neighbors will soon be firing their guns to celebrate. You couldn't sleep through that racket anyway. If James were home, he'd be shooting his gun to join in the fun."

Christmas! Rising Fawn blinked. She'd thought the ceremony at the church was Christmas.

"Hurry along now—it's the birthday of the Christ Child. Come and help me get ready."

Rising Fawn eased out of her trundle bed and went to the hearth. Although she didn't speak, she was smiling. If it were the Christ Child's birthday, she thought, perhaps someone would tell the rest of his story. And there was to be a feast after all. As the Woman lifted the lid of each pot, Rising Fawn leaned to smell the steam: peas, greens, potatoes, sweet apples with dumplings—and a guinea hen roasting on the spit.

"James will be home from the store by dusk," the Woman said. "We have a sight of chores to do. I haven't even gotten out my mother's linen cloth for the table yet. I brought it all the way from Mecklenburg, North Carolina, and that's been 'most ten years ago. We'll use the blue crockery plates too, instead of the pewter ones. Hurry now and get dressed."

The plank floor was cold to her feet, so Rising Fawn trotted across it quickly, smiling at the quarrelsome cluck of the hens who didn't like such sharp sounds above them. She came to the peg on the wall where she'd hung her clothes...and stopped. On the peg was her red dress—freshly washed, pieced, and mended neatly at the shoulder with a scrap of woolsey. On the floor were her moccasins, set side by side.

She looked back. The Woman had turned again to her cooking. Putting on the dress and moccasins, Rising Fawn went to stand beside her, shy with pleasure. The Woman looked down at her. "Mind you, it's just for today, just for Christmas." But her voice had a cheerful lilt. "Come now, we have work to do."

Rising Fawn enjoyed helping her. While the Woman held up one of the floor planks, Rising Fawn shooed two hens from their nests and gathered the warm, brown eggs. With a pine branch, she swept the floor, pushing the dust into the narrow cracks between the planks onto the earth beneath. The constant swishing warmed the pine, and in the tang of it, Rising Fawn smelled the familiar, comforting scent of the Grandmother.

"When you've finished sweeping, child, come help me make the corn bread," the Woman said. On the plank table, the Woman put a bowl of shucked corn that had been soaked in water. Rising Fawn dried each cob with a cloth. Into another bowl, the Woman put a piece of tin punctured with nail holes.

As she scraped a cob against the rough side, coarse meal sifted through. Rising Fawn watched it mounding and picked out random kernels that popped off whole. She licked the sweet meal off one, then held the kernel in her palm. It was different from Indian corn—white, large, and rather flat, with one end tapering. But in the center, she saw its heart, pale ivory and shaped like a flame. She closed her hand around it. "It is a sacred task to carry seeds for the people," her mother had said. But Rising Fawn knew her people would go to the new land without her. Her seeds would never be planted there. And though she had tried to be still and listen to the wisdom within, as the Grandmother had taught her, the Great Spirit had not spoken. It was not yet time to come forth.

The Woman had stopped stirring the corn bread. Looking up, Rising Fawn saw that she was watching her, with an expression curious and tender. "Child, can you show me now...what is in the pouch?"

Slowly, Rising Fawn opened her hand. The Woman touched the kernel, then the pouch. "Do you mean to tell me, it's filled with seed corn? Just seed corn?" When Rising Fawn nodded, the Woman smiled, as if she were bewildered and at the same time immensely relieved.

At dusk, when the Man's wagon rumbled into the clearing, Rising Fawn opened the door for him. The air was cold, the wind quiet. Beyond the web of branches in the woods, a full moon was rising. The Man walked slowly toward the door. "Well, now. It's mighty heartening to have you greet me. I see you're wearing your Indian dress—red is a good present for a brown-eyed girl. I've brought you a present too...for after supper." When the dishes had been done and the cloth folded away, Rising Fawn sat on her blanket by the hearth, facing the Man and Woman, who had drawn their chairs, side by side, within the circle of firelight.

"Christmas gift!" From his pocket, the Man drew out two things Rising Fawn had never seen before. One was shaped like a harvest moon, small, the color of pumpkins. "This is an orange," he said, "and this…is a stick of peppermint candy. When you're ready to eat them, I'll show you how to cut a hole in the orange and suck the juice up through the peppermint."

Rising Fawn took the gifts. She smelled the orange, then tasted the candy, following the red stripes with the tip of her tongue. She wanted to save the treats, make them last as long as possible. She wished she had something to give the Man and the Woman. The Woman must have sensed her wish, for she said, "Child, we want to love you and raise you for our own. If you want to give us a gift, speak to us. Tell us your name—just your name. That would be a beginning…"

When Rising Fawn drew back, the Woman patted her hand. "Never mind. I know you'll speak to us some day, in your own good time…For now, why don't you help me fix the Christmas candle in the window? We put it there for the Christ Child. Do you remember his story? Brother Owen told it at church."

Rising Fawn shook her head. All she remembered was that a great star appeared in the sky to show the people that the Christ Child had come to earth. But Brother Owen had left the story half-told. "The Great Spirit has made all things in harmony and the wisdom of the Great Spirit is within each thing," said the Grandmother. But who could find the wisdom in half a story? Rising Fawn was eager to hear all of it, and she smiled at the Woman to let her know.

"She's forgotten the story, James. But she wants to hear it again. Why don't you tell her…you know how to talk to her better than I do."

The Man rubbed his beard, then leaned forward with his elbows resting on his knees. "I don't know my letters, so I can't read it to you from the Bible. I'll just have to tell it to you plain.

"As you have cause enough to know, some people are set on being mean. But God...the Great Spirit...wants all his people to love each other and live in peace. So, he sent his son to show us how to do it. But he sent him as a little child...like a little candle in the dark, so to speak. And he sent him to a family—a man and a woman—because a child can't hardly make it in this world without a family. The Christ Child came down to earth at Christmas..."

"And that's why we put a candle in the window," the Woman said, "so when the Christ Child's spirit passes, he will see it and know he is welcome. It's a way of inviting love to come in."

"Sometimes he comes in the form of his own spirit," the Man went on. "And sometimes he comes in the form of a stranger—maybe like you've come to us..."

Rising Fawn had been listening intently, with the seed pouch pressed against her cheek. She felt the wisdom in the story, but a clear understanding was slow to come. She was still mulling over it as she put the tallow candle in its pewter holder and set it on the windowsill. The Woman lit a twig at the fire and brought it to the window. "Here, child. You light the candle..."

As Rising Fawn touched the burning twig to the wick, she thought of the Christ Child...of her own wandering...of her own hearth where the fire was kindled every year from the source of all life...

When the Woman moved back to her seat at the hearth, Rising Fawn barely heard the rustle of skirts, the creak of the chair. The candle flame was drawing her spirit-eyes and spirit-ears into its tiny light...and beyond, for the windowpane seemed to cast its reflection outside where it flickered like a seed of fire in the lap of night.

When the Man stirred the embering logs, the window also reflected the leaping flames. Rising Fawn watched them blaze brighter and larger around the candle's light. Many flames, one fire. Like the life of the seed caught in the shell of the corn, she stood watching the fire within the fire, and she felt its light kindled within her. Ablaze with recognition, she knew this was like Loak Mosholi, when each family in the clan kindled its cabin fire with a burning brand carried from the sacred fire. Each family was a flame within the flame. They were all people of one fire, one spirit. In a way she could not quite explain, Rising Fawn understood that she herself contained a tiny flame from which she and her people would draw strength. It was a flame that flowed from the source of all fires and all waters.

As her gaze deepened, she saw the smaller flame move in a silence so deep that she felt the wisdom within her rise and the Great Spirit began to speak—not in words, but in images. She dared not move, and her body-ears told Rising Fawn a patient and loving silence had fallen upon the room behind her.

From the heart of the candle flame, Rising Fawn saw the Grandmother's gnarled hands slowly unfold and spread like a wide cup to hold the sacred flame.

She saw the faces of the Man and the Woman and felt their love flow through the Grandmother's fingers into the firelight around her, warm as the earth.

She saw a russet kernel of corn. Its tough shell began to part. As a tendril root stretched down toward the earth, the slender sprout pushed upward—unfolding a tiny gleaming leaf.

She understood that her spirit was safe. She understood

34

also that she too would always carry seeds for her people, but that her seeds would come forth in this new land.

Quietly, she felt a new confidence and a deep relief that there was to be a time for her to come forth, like the flame within the seed had come forth. She turned around and moved close to the Man and the Woman, who had been watching her. They sat still, expectant. Rising Fawn folded one small hand around the Man's rough knuckles, and the other she placed within the upturned palm of the Woman. In a soft voice she said,

"My name is Rising Fawn."

Marilou Awiakta, a poet, storyteller, and essayist, has been active in Native American issues for most of her professional life. Born in Knoxville, Tennessee, and brought up in the Federal Nuclear Research community of Oak Ridge, Awiakta creates a unique weaving of her Cherokee/Appalachian heritages with science to express her basic theme: respect for the web of life. Her work appears in many national and international anthologies. She is the author of *Abiding Appalachia: Where Mountain and Atom Meet* and *Selu: Seeking the Corn Mother's Wisdom*, which was a 1994 Quality Paperback Book Club Selection. In 1989, Awiakta received the Distinguished Tennessee Writer Award. Her life and work are profiled in The Oxford's Companion to Women's Writing in the United States. The U.S. Information Agency chose *Rising Fawn and the Fire Mystery* and *Abiding Appalachia* for the world tour of their culture centers.

Awiakta lives in Memphis where she was a founder of the Native American Intertribal Association.

Beverly Bringle, a native of Covington, Tennessee, is of Choctaw descent. As a child, her great-grandfather endured the infamy of the Removal along the Trail of Tears. Bringle, who holds a master of fine arts degree from the University of Guanajuato, now lives in Concord, Massachusetts. She has exhibited both in Mexico and the United States.

CHI PISA LA CHIKE:
AN IRISHMAN'S PROMISE

Dianna Street

Not all were Choctaw who walked the trail, who suffered and lost.

Religion, stickball games, and an errant guide blend together in this tale of an Irishman's walk. With a Choctaw wife and five children, he makes a crucial decision along with three hundred other men. The family separates for a time, and he faces the uncertainty of whether they will all live to be together again.

Chi Pisa La Chike:
An Irishman's Promise

Dianna Street

"*Chi pisa la chike.*" Thomas didn't hold back. He kissed his wife with a passion he knew would embarrass as much as delight. "I will see you again. Be safe."

"We will." Tears formed in Eve's dark eyes.

He hugged his daughter, Harriet. "Help your Ma, take care of your brother and sister." It was an enormous load to put on the shoulders of an eight-year-old girl but there was no other option. Precious little had been his choice over the past few days.

"I will, Da." Harriet's voice cracked. Thomas watched her straighten her shoulders and look him in the eyes. She inherited that Irish pride from him. "Don't worry, we will be fine."

He managed a kiss on the top of Joel's head before the energetic four-year-old bounded off after a bug. Thomas nuzzled the newest member of their family, a three-month-old girl, Amanda. He looked into the eyes of his Choctaw bride, stroking her strong face. She blushed. He couldn't keep the mischievous smile from his face. Open displays of affection always embarrassed Eve.

Thomas scanned the shabby tent city they had built on the border of Vicksburg, Mississippi, and said a silent prayer of thanksgiving that the family wouldn't be there much longer. Army steamboats would arrive soon to take them to Camden, Arkansas, before the weather turned bad.

Thomas was the last one to step onto the steamboat bound for the west side of the Mississippi River. Their other two young sons, Joseph and Robert, were waiting on deck. The boys turned, a perfect mimic of the older men, and watched with him as the cold water stretched between them and those left behind. Thomas put a hand on the boys' shoulders and gave them a reassuring squeeze. The journey to the new Choctaw land had begun. At the end of this trail they would be men.

Robert and Joseph left the railing, running along and between the cords of wood stacked around the deck, toward the engine and boiler. Joseph was in the lead, but Robert was not far behind his younger brother. Thomas's stomach twisted in knots, thinking of Eve facing the long trip ahead with three small children.

"Da," Robert whispered, waving him over.

Thomas moved next to the cordwood and his son. Robert pulled his father down so they were sitting on the deck out of sight of Captain Brown who was having an animated conversation with the guide, Mr. Thatcher.

"But the map shows Monroe to be here." Captain Brown pointed to the map.

"The map is wrong." Thatcher leaned his lanky frame against the stacked wood.

"These were done by the military academy at West Point. I assure you, Mr. Thatcher, they are accurate."

"One mistake on paper," he paused to fill his cheek with tobacco, "can move a mountain."

"You will follow orders and your orders are to follow this map. You will meet up with Armstrong's men in Monroe and together get these men to Camden in two weeks."

"They'll be there."

Benjamin, a longtime friend, sat down beside Thomas. "Pushmataha has taken hunting parties to the territory President Jackson had promised the People. He called it the land of death."

Thomas rested his head against the wood. "And promised we could have it 'as long as grass grows and water runs.' Is that supposed to be a blessing or curse?"

"I guess that depends on who you are. The government got some of the best farmland in Mississippi, and we get...God only knows what we're getting." Benjamin stood and walked to a gathering of the elders.

A sudden chill in the air distracted Thomas from darker thoughts. The wind said it would soon rain. He looked around the deck and noticed similar expressions reflecting his. Thomas hoped to be on the other side of the river when rain fell.

They had been given two weeks to bring in their harvest and prepare for the journey. Four days later, when the family sat down for the evening meal, the soldiers arrived. They were forced, unprepared, from the only home their children had known. Corn cribs left full, clothes and blankets still hung on the line, dinner sitting on the table. The government representatives spoke to them as children, reserving disdain for Thomas, his fair skin and red hair igniting their Irish bigotry. "Don't worry, you will be provided for. Move quickly," they badgered. Too often the white man had gone back on his word.

Thomas chuckled out loud as he moved back to the railing. How odd he no longer saw himself as a white man.

As the ferry reached the far side, Thomas's thoughts moved to the deal he'd made, causing him to leave Eve and the three youngest children on the other side.

The day after arriving in Vicksburg, General Gaines sent soldiers into the camp asking the men to voluntarily march instead of riding the overloaded steamboats to Camden. In an effort to ease the conscience of the Bureau of Indian Affairs agents, the men were offered ten gold coins, a rifle, three months' worth of powder and ammunition, and a guide. What was clear was it wasn't a choice. Thomas still felt he shouldn't have left.

Thunder rumbled in the distance as the men stepped off the boat. Captain Brown's men handed out the promised payment while he spoke from the ferry deck. "Gentlemen. This is your guide, Mr. Thatcher. Follow him and you will be reunited with your families in Camden. Godspeed." Lightning flashed as the soldiers boarded the ferry for the return trip.

"Let's move before the rain mires our route," Thatcher bellowed, turning his face to the west. Three hundred men fell into a silent line behind him.

That night a storm came roaring in. Lightning split the sky as thunder shook the trees. It wasn't long before Thomas and the boys' meager shelter, a rough lean-to made from blankets with a rock outcropping at their backs, allowed the pounding rain to turn small leaks into steady streams. Thomas pulled the boys close and shared the last blanket. There would be no fire in this camp tonight. Robert took dried meat and fruit from the bag and handed it to Joseph and Thomas.

While they ate, Thomas hummed *Vba Isht Tola, Give Me Christ, Or Else I Die.* It was Eve's favorite hymn and humming it made him feel close to her and to God. In Vicksburg, she would have a dry tent to sleep in and a hot meal. There wasn't much for him to do except endure and try to get some rest.

The rain continued into morning, mud sucking at their feet. Diseases that came among them in Vicksburg dogged their steps. By force of will they kept a steady pace, resting only when necessary and to bury their dead, which was far too often. There would be no game tonight; maybe the fishing would be better. But when they reached the swollen river the hope of fresh food died. A tangle of shrubs and trees lined the north side of the flooded banks, while the south turned sharply out of sight.

"We'll have to cross here," Mr. Thatcher said.

"Shouldn't we look for a better place?" Thomas asked and others nodded their heads in agreement.

"You won't find anything better for twenty miles either side."

Thomas walked upstream until he was out of sight of the resting men and could go no farther. But there was a debris accumulation that might allow the men to scramble across. It would not be safe if the river continued to swell. But if he could prove to Thatcher it was stable enough now, it could give them a safe passage. Thomas returned, arriving in time to see Thatcher leading the group into the flood waters. Thomas waded in, waist deep, and caught up with Joseph just as he slipped and went under. Thomas managed to catch hold of his shirt and pulled him close. He searched in panic for Robert. Benjamin was helping the twelve-year-old up the steep bank. Thomas clung to Joseph until they reached the other side, where Benjamin and Robert held out hands to help them up.

Thatcher ordered them to march forward. Wet clothes clinging to him, Thomas's mind drifted once again to Eve. He hummed *Vba Isht Tola, Give Me Christ, Or Else I Die* and remembering the joy in her voice eased his anger for the *ofi* leading them. To his surprise Robert and Joseph were humming, too. It made him smile. Joseph was most like his mother, dark eyes and hair with the voice of an angel. Robert was more like himself, green eyes and fair complexion and flaming red hair. Both boys had her deep and trusting faith. Long ago, Thomas had left the Catholic Church and its trappings behind with his mother in Virginia. Eve taught him who Jesus was through rich faith and simple belief.

Thomas raised his eyes to heaven and whispered, "Father in heaven protect and care for my family while they are away from me."

At sunset Thatcher announced, "We'll camp here tonight."

The rain had not let up. There would be no fire, no game, and little or no shelter. Dinner would be more dried meat and fruit. Robert and Joseph had cut red maple branches, shaping them into a shelter. Thomas helped them and hung the canteens on an outstretched limb to catch fresh water before he moved out of the rain.

"Your mother is not here to tell a story so you'll have to listen to mine." Thomas grinned. Eve told the family histories at night, but like a good Irishman he could spin a yarn as well as any.

"My parents were born in Derry, Ireland. They made a fair amount of money in the linen trade, but the family tired of Protestant interference in their religion. So they took it upon themselves to leave their homeland and start new." Thomas passed dried meat and fruit to his sons. "It took three curraghs to get them across to Liverpool. From there they bought passage to the New World. It was a long and rough trip but they finally made it to Jamestown."

A puzzled look crossed Joseph's face.

"That's in Virginia." Thomas paused long enough to drink water from the canteen. "Once there, they learned the sugar business and in a few years managed the Buckner family plantation. Some Algonquians traded with the plantation, and they taught me how to trap and trade in furs. I was restless and after some time I left. Traveling, following the game, I ended up in Mississippi." Thomas looked at the rain, and then at his boys. "Go to sleep. I'll tell you more tomorrow night."

It was a grey morning but thankfully the hard rain had stopped in the middle of the night. A light drizzle persisted, leaving the group in a melancholy mood. Robert and Joseph followed behind Thomas. As they walked, Thomas hummed and Joseph sang in English.

Gracious Lord, incline Thine ear;
My request vouchsafe to hear;
Hear my never-ceasing cry;
Give me Christ, or else I die.

Wealth and honor I disdain,
Earthly comforts, Lord, are vain;
These can never satisfy:
Give me Christ, or else I die.

They stopped for a rest and food at the edge of a bog, allowing those burying the dead to catch up. The slow drizzle had turned into a slow steady rain, north winds raced through their group leaving a bitter chill. Joseph's face was pale, making the dark circles under his eyes stand out, but he hadn't complained of an illness.

Thomas sat on the log next to him. "Eat something," he coaxed.

"Thanks," Joseph said with a thin smile, placing the dried meat between his lips.

"Da, how long until we reach Camden?" Robert asked.

"Another week. We'll meet your mother and the rest of the family at John Camden's Post and from there we'll go to Washington. The rest of the trip is a simple ride on the river to Fort Towson. At Doaksville, we'll start the new Choctaw Nation."

"The Land of Death," Robert added.

"No, the Choctaw Nation. Pushmataha may have been right when he called it that but we will thrive there and make it into a great nation."

"How can you be so sure?" Robert asked.

"Because I have faith in our people and in God above." With that they settled into a comfortable quiet, and for a time rested.

All too soon they had to be on their way. Thomas handed the canteen to Joseph who then handed it to Robert without drinking from it. After Robert had his fill he passed it back. "Joseph, you should drink." Thomas once again offered the canteen to Joseph.

"I'm not thirsty. Maybe later."

Thomas took the canteen and held it above his head to refill it with fresh rain water. While they walked, Joseph sang in English while the others followed in Choctaw.

The deer trail turned into a thick river of mud. Each step was an attempt to break free from the earth before it pulled them under. They were mud people and so many on this journey had been buried in it that it seemed as if the Creator wanted them to return to the mud. But they continued to the sound of the hymn so close to their hearts, *Vba Isht Tola, Give Me Christ, Or Else I Die.*

> *All unholy and unclean,*
> *I am weighted by my sin;*
> *On thy mercy I rely;*
> *Give me Christ, or else I die.*

> *Thou dost freely save the lost;*
> *In Thy grace alone I trust;*
> *With my earnest plea comply;*
> *Give me Christ, or else I die.*

> *All unholy and unclean,*
> *I am weighted by my sin;*
> *On thy mercy I rely;*
> *Give me Christ, or else I die.*

It was hard to tell the night from the day with this kind of weather. When they stopped, once again the boys pulled branches to form a shelter. They wouldn't be dry but at least they wouldn't have water falling on them while they slept. Thomas scouted around for something to supplement their meager ration of dried meat and water. He couldn't find more than a few berries. On his way back to the camp he saw Mr. Thatcher roaming the woods with a map, muttering, but Thomas was too far away to hear what he was saying.

When he returned to camp, Joseph was sitting on a log with his hands wrapped around himself. "What is the matter?" Thomas asked, feeling the boy's head.

"My stomach is cramping."

"How much water have you had?"

"Not much, every time I drank I needed to go...I was falling behind."

"Do what you need to, we will stay together." Thomas reached into his bag and pulled out a small flask. He poured a dark syrup into the canteen and mixed it with the water. "Drink this elderberry water and maybe you'll feel better in the morning." He pushed Joseph's hair out of his eyes. The boy felt warm to him. Dysentery, diphtheria, and cholera ran rampant whenever the white man came among the people. It was too soon to tell which Joseph had; with no cough Thomas didn't think it was diphtheria. Elderberry would work for now and tomorrow he would look for help from a willow tree.

Once again the rains left them with no campfire and the last of the rations they brought with them. Tomorrow they would have to hunt or fish. Thomas hung the canteen from the shelter. At least they would have fresh water.

"Da, what will happen if we can't find food tomorrow?" Robert asked.

"God will provide," Thomas said with a smile. "Do you want to hear another story tonight?" Both boys nodded. Lightning cracked the air, the sound reminding him of the first *toli* he attended.

The clacking of sticks rang above the roar of the gathered clans. Wagons, tents, and the ponies of thousands of spectators and players surrounded the mile-long clearing. The festival atmosphere was laced with tension from the unresolved dispute the game was to settle. Elders on the sidelines made bets and yelled instructions to the players. The excitement was infectious.

A woman walked toward Thomas. The sun shone on her dark hair with such intensity it made his heart skip a beat. She asked, "Why did you not play?"

Thomas's mouth went dry and his head spun.

She blew out a breath in disgust. Turning, her hair fanned out like a halo. She snatched up her sticks and ran onto the field. The women's game was in full swing, wrestling and fighting dominating the area around the goal post. With speed and grace she caught the ball from the air and charged shouting, "*Hokli Ho!*" She was fearless. But before she could complete her throw she was grabbed from behind and thrown to the ground. Thomas's fists were clenching at his side.

"She loves to play," a voice said at his side. "I had too many sons before I had a daughter."

Thomas looked into the proud eyes of the old man standing next to him and recognized him as Tobaca Apukshunnubbee. "How can you not worry about her out there?" he asked the chief.

"I worry. I worry she'll never find a husband strong enough for her."

The chief's daughter dove for the legs of a woman making a run at the goal post. As they fell, she used her own momentum to come back up to her knees, driving an elbow into her opponent's stomach. The other woman gasped and coughed but got up quicker than Thomas thought possible. The women were off and running after another player.

Thomas felt Tobaca's eye evaluating him. "Come to our tent tonight. At dinner toss this to her." He handed Thomas a smooth black river stone. "Be sure she sees where it came from."

"Then what?"

"If she stomps off…" He shrugged his shoulders.

Thomas couldn't take his eyes off the chief's daughter. "If she doesn't?"

"Come back in a month for the wedding."

Thomas froze, feeling the blood drain from his face. "I don't know if I'm ready…," he stammered. "A wife…I just left my own da and ma."

Tobaca's laugh resonated in his soul and Thomas knew the old man was right; she would be his wife.

"I'll tell you about the first time I met your mother." Thomas moved farther into the shelter and pulled the boys close.

The next morning the rain stopped. It was November, and with the cold sun came the wind. The forest had turned to swamp. Thomas walked away from the camp in search of willow. He saw Mr. Thatcher walking east, while reading a map with pack and bedroll on his back. "Good morning, Mr. Thatcher."

"Good morning," he said, startled.

"Are we leaving?" Thomas pointed to Thatcher's full pack.

"No, just doing a little scouting. Go back to camp and I'll be there soon."

"How much longer until we reach Camden?"

"What? Oh, two, three days at the most, it's just west and north of here. Go back to camp before you get lost," he said, punctuating his words with tobacco spit.

"Thank you." Thomas set out to find willow. He turned back to watch Thatcher walk east. Their party had been traveling south instead of north, to avoid what Thatcher had called harsh terrain. It seemed to Thomas they were just getting deeper and deeper into it. He suspected Mr. Thatcher was confused, or lost.

After returning to camp with the bark, he gathered some of the other men and spoke to them about this. They agreed with his conclusions and planned to talk to Mr. Thatcher when he returned. They waited most of the day, but their guide had disappeared. The men used the time to hunt the woods for game, build fires that could stay lit, tend to the sick, and get some much needed rest. As the sun set, the men sat around a central fire and discussed their next move.

Thomas was the first to speak. "He said Camden is northwest of here. I suggest we walk in that direction."

One of the elders spoke up. "We don't know where we are. How can we trust his directions are right? For that matter, how can we be sure which way is back?"

Thomas took a long drink from his canteen, giving himself time to think about what was said. "We can't stay here, so we either need to go forward or backward. Going back will only force us to make this trip again and I for one don't want that."

They all agreed.

The next morning dawned bright and cold as the party broke camp and moved northwest. The cold air did little to dry the ground and it wasn't long before they were walking waist deep in the swamp, struggling through the trails they made. Thomas looked around at those walking with him. The journey began with more than three hundred men; so far one hundred and thirteen of them would never finish. Benjamin, who had helped on the farm since before his children were born, said he heard an owl last night and that death was coming for him. The look on Benjamin's face said it would be soon. Thomas also feared Joseph would not see the end of this trail. Joseph started to sing, *Vba Isht Tola, Give Me Christ, Or Else I Die.*

> *Thou hast promised to forgive*
> *All who in thy Son believe;*
> *Lord, I know Thou cannot lie;*
> *Give me Christ, or else I die.*

> *All unholy and unclean,*
> *I am weighted by my sin;*
> *On thy mercy I rely;*
> *Give me Christ, or else I die.*

Over and over Joseph sang first in English then in Choctaw, a prayer, pushing them onward with rhythm, their bare feet smacking the mud to the beat. When Joseph could sing no more another took up the song, and then another until it was time to stop for the night. Joseph's symptoms were worse. It was clear he had dysentery and it pained Thomas to see his son suffering. Elderberry and willow helped, but he needed to be in a warm, dry place as well.

That night as the men gathered in small groups to eat, their general mood had lightened. They knew the situation and how dire it was, but today Joseph reminded them of whose hands they rested in.

Joseph slumped against a tree. As Robert and Thomas lashed the shelter together, Robert whispered to his father, "Benjamin was buried an hour ago."

They both looked toward Joseph. "We are doing all we can. Just pray. Move your brother inside please."

Thomas hung the canteen on the shelter and moved inside.

"Tonight I'm going to tell you about how your mother learned medicine and what she taught me. When your mother was a little girl she wandered off into the woods and was gone for days. Her family had given her up as dead when she walked back into the village with no real explanation of where she had been. She told me that a little man had found her in the woods and taught her about herbs, berries, and plants. He then taught her how to mix them into medicines. This is why she is a healer. She taught me how to make the elderberry syrup and which willow bark is the best to relieve pain as well as how to prepare it. Just as she is teaching Harriet, and someday Amanda…"

Joseph interrupted, "Why is she only teaching my sisters?"

Thomas smiled. "Your mother said after teaching me, girls would be much easier. But if you were to ask her I'm…" Thomas looked up as a white man walked into camp.

"*Halito*," the man said. Everyone acknowledged his Choctaw greeting. "Where is Thatcher?"

Thomas left his sons and walked toward the stranger. "Don't know, left four days ago."

"You know you were supposed to be at Monroe two weeks ago?"

"Yes, you know the way?"

"My name is John Mullins." He stuck out his hand. "I was sent to find you and bring you in."

Thomas shook his hand. "How far off are we?"

"I'd say about as far away as you can get, another day and you'd be in New Orleans. We'll get you turned around and be in Monroe in no time at all."

"We've been walking for three weeks and haven't gone the seventy-seven miles to Monroe?"

"It looks like you've gotten a mite lost. Good news is I'll have you in Monroe in three days and in Camden with your families in another week."

The next morning they walked with John Mullins in the lead. The men had a desperate sense of hope even as the cold north wind blew in their faces. Joseph was not getting better. Thomas had enough elderberry syrup to maintain Joseph the remainder of the trip, if this guide could be trusted. But even if he couldn't, Thomas knew where they were and God willing they would make it before the rest of his family was to be taken along the Red River to Doaksville.

In a tent city that occupied the outer edges of Camden, Arkansas, Robert left Thomas and Joseph behind to find his mother. Thomas set Joseph down, the boy pale and exhausted, and threw back tent flap after tent flap asking those he saw about the rest of his family. He stumbled into the tent of an elder woman, Neakiat.

"Have you seen Eve?"

"They stopped to bury their dead. I have not seen them since," the old woman croaked.

Thomas's world went out of focus, his knees buckled, but he didn't fall. It took all his strength to walk back to his son. Thomas's mind drifted back to his wedding day and the day each of his children was born. His life passed with sudden clarity—time was too short. His family was slipping through his fingers. Dark spots danced before his eyes and Thomas took several deep breaths until they passed.

Robert came running between the tents. "I've found them!"

Thomas pulled Joseph's arm around his neck and together they stumbled behind Robert. When they reached the open flap, Thomas stopped, afraid of what was on the other side. He lunged into the darkened interior and saw the deep brown eyes of Eve. He gasped. "Chi pisa la chike, I told you I'd see you again."

She threw herself into his arms and sobbed, holding him tight. The unexpected display of emotion in his normally constrained wife moved him to tears. She pushed back from him, looking at her sons. Thomas helped Joseph to the floor and watched as Eve went to work caring for him. Thomas picked up Joel and Harriet, holding them close. "I missed you, Da," Harriet whispered as she nestled against his neck.

"I missed you too." Looking at Eve, he asked, "Where is the baby?"

"We buried her under a sycamore tree." Tears filled her eyes. "I have to find more elderberries for Joseph." Eve rushed out, sobbing.

Harriet cried, "They tried to hurt Joel, Da. The soldiers told us he was going too slow, too little to keep up; we needed to let him go. They were going to beat him against a tree like Margaret Folsom's boy. Ma and I ran for the woods. We walked in the shadows behind everyone else until we made it here." He could feel her shuddering as she told him of their trip west. He sobbed inside himself at the loss of his baby Amanda. But he knew she was resting in peace.

That night, after the evening meal, Eve moved between her husband and children, caring for them. Thomas held Joel and Harriet until they fell asleep, listening to his wife's sweet voice as she hummed her favorite hymn. He offered up a silent prayer of thanks that his family was healing and so was he.

A native of Oklahoma, **Dianna Street** can trace her Choctaw heritage to Chief Tobaca Apukshunnubbee. *Chi Pisa La Chike: An Irishman's Promise* chronicles her great-great-great-great grandfather, Thomas Everidge, and his trial on the Trail of Tears. Dianna is the author of several published short stories in e-zines and print media. Now living in Edmond, Oklahoma, she writes in multiple genres and is currently working on a horror anthology and a historical romance.

SOMEWHERE,

WILLIAM WALLACE SMILED

James Masters

Many heroes lived before Agamemnon, but they are unwept and unknown because they had no poet to sing of them.—Horace

This sensitive and lyrical piece takes us on a journey of the heart, of the mind, of the soul. Of the Choctaw way.

Somewhere,

William Wallace Smiled

James Masters

This is a story of a story of a story. But I've said too much!
It's a curious little tale about a Choctaw brave called
Wild-at-Heart.

I confess before going any further that I'm uncertain
exactly where William Wallace, so prominently featured in the
title of this story, fits in. Wallace, you may remember, was the
Scotsman who hacked his way through the English armies of
Edward Longshanks, fighting for a free Scotland in the twelve
hundreds. His peasant army, undisciplined and vastly out-
numbered, fought battle after ferocious battle, finally routing
the well-armed, highly trained English soldiers at Stirling
Bridge. When finally he was captured, he was tortured, hanged,
drawn and quartered, eviscerated and beheaded. It wasn't

enough. He died, but it was not in vain. Someone saw, someone remembered, and someone told the story. Nine years later, those battered and bloodied men who had fought and bled with him stormed the fields of Bannockburn and, when the fighting ended, they were free. Wallace's story did what all great stories do—it changed those who heard it—and of those there were many for it was told down through the ages by poets and warriors alike. The story of the rebel hero, his courage in life and death, was simply unstoppable.

It's a little confusing where the Scottish hero, born five hundred years before our tale begins, fits into our story, but as he's right there in the title I felt I should mention him early on. And I'll certainly try to work him into the story later, even if it's the last thing I do. Though you probably will have forgotten all about him by then.

Wild-at-Heart always wore a foolish, lopsided grin, was too shy for this world, and early on became the butt of jokes. He was too big for his age. His hands were too big for the ends of his arms. His features were noteworthy in that every item was out of proportion. He never talked, and if he did, he always went away thinking he had said the wrong thing and so talked less and less. It became common to include him in any story about odd goings-on and his name became synonymous with foolishness among Indians and settlers alike. His most common thing to say when he did talk was, "You're funnin' me," and, in fact, they always were. He carried with him in his broad face and ungainly form so much blushing embarrassment he always seemed as if he had just come from doing something foolish and was on his way to do something foolish.

By the time he was a grown man and his contemporaries had dropped the ugly, hurtful teasing—it gave way to the pitiful shake of the head at the poor, hapless fellow—a new generation of youth had come along to poke fun.

Laugh as they might at his odd ways, no one could question his courage. When he was seventeen, on the banks of the swollen Pascagoula River, he had stood his ground before an overwhelming band of Creeks and fought them one by one like Horatius at Rome, until the braves on the other side destroyed the bridge leading to the Choctaw camp, preventing the Creeks from crossing. When Wild-at-Heart threw himself into the raging river and finally emerged safely on the other side, the Creeks, like Horatius's enemies before them, could not help but cheer.

This might have changed the estimate of the boy but he never talked of the event. The one time he was persuaded of it by a gaggle of girls he disintegrated into such stammering and stuttering, they laughed him to derision.

His mother was one of the first of the Choctaws to pay heed to the Presbyterian missionaries and Wild-at-Heart got sprinkled himself though everyone remarked he was as foolish the day after as the day before.

He took to spending his time outdoors; that was the life he loved. He was better with animals than with people. His irregular ways didn't bother them and his awkwardness was redeemed by his gentle nature. Wild-at-Heart's one friend was his cousin, Peter Gardner, a handsome boy of sixteen with dark, flashing eyes. Peter had gone to one of the missionary schools, had read more books than any two judges and would recite quotations even if no one asked him to. He was eloquent. He talked like a character from a book. Sometimes even he didn't know what he meant.

"My favorite quotation?" Peter said one day, as if someone had inquired. He gazed into the distance like a poet and saw a thousand years into the past and halfway around the world. "It was brave Ulister who said, 'And as the battle reached its close I realized, life is un-understandable, it's just to be lived.' "

Wild-at-Heart knew only one quote and he surprised even himself by shyly, gruffly reciting it now. It was the longest sentence he uttered in his lifetime. "Let us sit on the ground and tell sad stories of the deaths of kings." He ached when he said it, though he did not know what came before or after.

Peter Gardner repeated the line and nodded in appreciation. He saw someone coming—it was Wild-at-Heart's mother—gave a comical grin and made the silly comment, "Your mother's hair looks like a cow slept in it."

It was a harmless enough thing to say, but it struck Wild-at-Heart oddly and for some reason that he could not fathom, he was enraged. He turned on Peter and swung his fist into the boy's face. It was the most singular occurrence in his life. So hard was the blow that it knocked Peter to the ground, crushed the left side of his face and killed him instantly.

And so our story begins in tragedy, when it could have been otherwise.

In older times, before the coming of the missionaries, the fate of a Choctaw who killed another man was left in the hands of the dead man's relatives. It was both their right and their duty to dispatch the killer and so avenge their kinsman. Whether the avenging blow came quickly or slowly, it came certainly.

While the murderer could have escaped, he was never known to do so. Such a cowardly act would have brought disgrace not only onto him but upon his family. If he did flee, the life of one of his male relatives would be forfeit instead. So he awaited his sure fate impassively, seeking no help nor expecting any, and the avenger went about his business without fear of being stopped by either friend or foe.

Shortly after the coming of the missionaries, the police force known as the Light Horsemen took over the duties of deciding an accused man's fate and the murderer was no longer left in the hands of the relatives of the dead man. There were no jails for none were needed. If, after a hearing of the evidence, a man was condemned by the Light Horse and told when and where to show up for his punishment, nothing on earth could keep him from that appointment. The Choctaws were singular in this obsession with keeping the law.

Brokenhearted, Wild-at-Heart picked up Peter's body and, stooped with shame, made the long walk to the home of Dolphie Gardner, Peter's father, where he stammered out what had happened, all the while holding the poor boy's body in his arms. "I'm awful sorry," he said over and over again. "Awful sorry."

Dolphie Gardner, an old man past seventy, was a gentle soul, not given to much talk, and his silent ways did not fail him now. He listened to Wild-at-Heart's recounting, took his son, and motioned that he might go.

Wild-at-Heart left Dolphie Gardner's and took himself to the Light Horsemen where he repeated his story in a few faltering words, none of them trying to lessen what he had done. There was no doubt of the outcome.

Henry Nowabbi, tall, thin, levelheaded, and Sonny Istubby, stout and amiable, had known Wild-at-Heart all their lives and were staggered by what he told them. "How did this happen?" Henry asked, shaking his head in disbelief.

"The woman," Wild-at-Heart always called his mother "the woman," "she says it's because I'm wild at heart."

"I always thought that meant you liked it outside better than in, fishing and hunting for bear, beaver and critters and such," Sonny said.

"I thought it, too," said Wild-at-Heart. He liked Sonny. In their youth when a group of boys had been pelting Wild-at-Heart with rocks, Sonny had thrown a piece of hard candy instead. Sonny had smiled secretly when Wild-at-Heart reached out his hand and caught it.

"Is there anyone else who can speak on this matter?" Henry asked.

Wild-at-Heart shook his head.

"Your own words condemn you," Henry said, not unkindly. "I see nothing else for it. You fix a day and a time."

One peculiarity of the Choctaw system of justice was that the condemned man might request a brief reprieve prior to his execution. The reason might be as crucial as harvesting the crops for his family to survive or as trifling as the desire to attend an upcoming dance or ball-play. The respite was granted, the condemned attended to the matter at hand, huge or slight, and then, at the appointed time, showed up to accept his punishment, even so severe a one as death.

Unaccustomed to seeking favors, Wild-at-Heart reluctantly made a request now, though it was not for himself he asked. He and his mother were to be part of the first removal of the Choctaws from Mississippi to the lands west of Arkansas.

"The woman's going to the new lands. It'll be a hard trip without me," he said apologetically.

Henry nodded. "Get her there," he said. "We'll do it then, out there."

After the hapless fellow had gone, Will Kemp stepped from the dark where he had been standing throughout this interview. Kemp was a hard, stern man, tough, unforgiving, and flawed beyond measure. He would have been lonesome in any company.

Henry turned to him. "You're in charge of the removal, Kemp?"

"One of the agents. Not in charge," Kemp said in his clipped way. "Same as you."

He had been conveying to the Light Horse details of the removal when Wild-at-Heart arrived.

"You'll be glad to see all of us gone, won't you?" Sonny said.

Kemp didn't deny it. He did not like the Choctaws. He had had rough dealings with those given to drink and pilfering, and had saddled the entire bunch with the same estimate. He did not abide weakness and had no truck with an addlepated fellow like Wild-at-Heart.

"That much time. That far away. He'll never show," he said now.

"What does it matter to you?" Sonny asked. "You didn't like Peter Gardner either, did you?"

"No," Kemp said. "I didn't like him either." He walked outside into the coming night.

Kemp was not optimistic about this western removal. There had been too much rain throughout the summer and fall, they were starting too late in the year, and there was something about the air that promised a raw, biting cold. He would be glad when it was over and they were gone.

Wild-at-Heart's mother, Anoni, was gentle and humble and always the last in line. She began life with no expectations and came from nowhere to be great, though only a few would ever know it. His father was a miscreant of cruel and severe disposition, long dead, and why she had married him no one could say, though I won't blame her if you won't. What would be the use?

She knew what had happened and sat waiting for her son to return from the Light Horse. It was, incongruously, the finest part of the day. The last fading rays of the sun fell horizontally into the house and turned everything they touched to gold. And it was beautiful then. But that time of day doesn't last long and the pale glow, unable to linger, reluctantly deserted the room little by little until finally the house was dark and silent. And still she sat and waited, with every irrational hope in heaven running through her mind. When Wild-at-Heart finally arrived she came to her feet desperate to hear what had transpired, yet did not want him to speak because she knew that once the words were loosed, they could not be undone.

"They'll wait a bit, 'til we get to the new lands," he said.

Her hopes had not prevailed.

The history of Indian removal in the United States is long and convoluted with more twists than the Mississippi River itself. It has heroes and scoundrels on both sides, profiteers, pragmatists, seers, visionaries, cutthroats, and that rascal Andrew Jackson. Briefly put, the federal government, egged on by the state and the settlers who craved the rich Mississippi farmland, pressured the Choctaws into a series of treaties giving up more and more of their ancient homeland until finally, with the Treaty of Dancing Rabbit Creek in 1830, they ceded the last ten million acres and, almost without realizing it, stunningly, the whole kit and caboodle was gone.

The treaty called for the Choctaws to be removed to the land west of Arkansas in three trips, the first two of which proved disastrous. The most severe blizzard in the history of the South coupled with torrential rains, swollen rivers, impenetrable swamps, bad planning, endless disagreements, shortages of rations, diphtheria, dysentery and the cholera conspired to quash any chance the Choctaws or removal agents had of making a success of the business. Of the 12,500 Choctaws who left Mississippi, there is no accurate count of how many perished along the way; there were too many to keep track.

In October of 1831, a group of two hundred Choctaws that included Wild-at-Heart, his mother and Dolphie Gardner, gathered along the Leaf River north of what would later become Hattiesburg. The treaty said the Choctaws had agreed to the removal, but that night told a different tale: the women covered their heads and wept and the men grieved in unnatural silence. They could not understand how they had come to this. They were trading all they had ever known for uncertain promises someone else had weaved for them.

"How will they treat Choctaws out there?" Wild-at-Heart shyly asked his mother that night, a question he had been pondering.

"As we show them to," she answered and hoped that she was right.

Sonny Istubby came by and said, "We'll leave soon as it's light."

It was all he had to say, but he didn't go. He stood there, a grown man looking lost and helpless, not knowing what to do until finally he shook his fist at nothing, and then, needing to say something but not knowing what to say, struggling desperately, settled for proclaiming loudly to no one in particular that he was born hardheaded, he had lived all his life hardheaded, and he could guarantee he would die hardheaded.

"I wouldn't put it past you," said Anoni with gentle good humor, and they were able to smile at that.

More than four thousand Choctaws left in that first removal; five hundred from the Northeastern district were sent to Memphis, while those from the Northwest and South set out for Vicksburg, to move west from there. Will Kemp proved the seer. Unremitting rains stretched the treacherous swamps fifty miles wide on both sides of the Mississippi. Brutal winds dropped snow and sleet endlessly. The mercury fell to zero and stayed there. The women were barefoot, the children wore little or nothing. Rivers were clogged with ice, the roads sat waist deep in mud and water, much of the terrain was impassible.

When the band coming from the Leaf reached a settlement south and east of Vicksburg, the news already had arrived that the Choctaws were bringing the cholera, when in fact it was the other way around. The disease was there already and the settlement would be ravaged and empty within a week.

The trail the Choctaws took ran beside an ancient stone wall, high as a man's head, running along the south side of the settlement, the only remnant of some long-abandoned plan to fortify the village. There was a gap in the wall that had once held a gate and it was there the frightened settlers gathered, intent on making certain no Choctaw entered. They stood back a hundred feet from the wall and called to the band to keep moving until one man, as if to give force to his words, picked up a rock and hurled it. It struck one of the Choctaws passing the opening with a thud. Another man picked up a rock and threw it, then another and another and in only a moment, every settler was hurling rocks.

The narrow, muddy, unforgiving trail, hemmed in by the wall on one side and impenetrable woods on the other, afforded the only way past the opening. The weary Choctaws no longer had it in them to hurry or even to try to avoid the stones; they simply ducked their heads and trudged forward. The settlers threw with a grim, steady monotony.

And then a man—big, hapless, foolish—stepped into the gap, and he stood there. He did not move on. He did not duck or cower or make himself small. Instead, he rose up to fill the gap. And he took the stones, one after another, every one meant for him, every one meant for those weary souls passing behind him.

The settlers saw what was happening and, oddly, perked up. Great Jehoshaphat, here was a target! They redoubled their efforts. One landed a solid blow, and he laughed. And then another and another, until a wild, hilarious laughter spread through the throng, though none of them could have said what they were laughing for. They whooped and hollered. They were positively lighthearted; they might have been at a carnival. Though the temperature was below freezing, one crooked old man past eighty took off his coat, the better to throw. His rock hit squarely and, for the first and only time in his life, he danced a jig. The cholera was forgotten. A girl hit the target and squealed. "Watch me," said one man. He took a running start and threw so hard he fell down. He got up laughing and wiped the mud off his knees. Two men grabbed arms and, no one knew why, hopped up and down.

The Choctaw, for his part, stood there. And he took it.

The barrage might have gone on forever but for an odd thing that happened. As if there were not comedy enough, a stray dog bounded into the clearing, positively ecstatic to be among the players and their doings. He yapped and ran in circles and no one could catch him, not the young boys who ran at him or those who kicked at him when he came near. But he would not retire from the scene. Finally, the dog saw the man standing in the gap in the wall. He ran and jumped up on him, wild with delight, laughing (if a dog can laugh), and shaking his tail so vigorously it was in danger of falling off. Wild-at-Heart, alone among the congregation, dropped to his knees and petted the dog with a singular joy, as if this were the friend he had been waiting to see.

Why this affected the settlers in such extraordinary fashion is difficult to say unless it had to do with the fact they were not wicked, only frightened. For whatever the reason, the old man let his arm go slack and the rock he held dropped. He didn't say a word, just picked up his coat, turned and trudged back through the mud toward the village. And one by one the others, as if dropping rocks was contagious, let their rocks slide from their hands. The whoops and catcalls ground to a halt; the only sound was the thud of rocks dropping dead into the mud. One by one they walked away. One fellow tried to keep the moment alive.

"Look here, look here," he called and threw two rocks at once. But the time for that had gone and no one turned to look. The foolish fellow hurried after the others and the only thing left in the clearing was the mud and the shame.

The battered and bloodied figure in the gap, embarrassed now without knowing why, hoped only that he had not done anything wrong, hoped no one noticed what he had done in case he had behaved foolishly and did not know it. In shy and clumsy fashion, he slid back into line. There was still a long way to go.

Once the removal parties reached Vicksburg, it was clear that the flooded roads would make it impossible to go west from the Mississippi by wagon so the agents went back to their original plan of using steamboats to go as far as they could into Arkansas by river. By the time boats were rounded up, weeks had passed, the rations that had been procured were gone and the Indians camped outside the town were starving and freezing. The number of dead mounted.

While the other groups had waited outside Vicksburg for the steamboats, Wild-at-Heart's party wandered, lost in the swamps. The desperate group, in danger of being left behind, marched two days without pause barefoot over the frozen terrain to reach the gathering place. All the other Choctaws were gone. One of the boats, the Talma, had been sent back for them but it would not wait. The river already was choked with ice and they could not suffer delay. This last boat would leave at dawn.

As soon as the demoralized band straggled into camp that night, frozen and exhausted, a long, drawn wail went up from one corner. Anoni's cousin, Baiyih, mortally ill herself, had been carried into camp and realized only when she awoke from a fever that her five-year-old was not there; she had been lost on the trail. There had been so many deaths, at this point the girl's only made one more. Going back to try to find her at night in the freezing cold was impossibly foolish. With the sub-zero weather, the rampant disease, the lack of provisions, missing the boat was a death sentence.

Wild-at-Heart was the last to enter camp. Anoni met him and told him the story of her cousin and the missing girl. She looked at him with a mother's eyes. He had never let her down before. He did not let her down now. Without a word he turned and started back the way he had come.

The removal agents shook their heads at the foolhardy fellow. The girl could not still be alive; he was consigning himself to the same fate.

Will Kemp, who had been put in charge of getting this group upriver, shouted at the back of the retreating figure: "The boat leaves at dawn! We wait for no one!"

More rain came that night. And then, more ice. The mercury passed zero. So far had the greedy river overflowed its bank, it was impossible to tell where it stopped and land began. The Choctaws were huddled on the only spot high enough to remain dry; all else was swamp; the dock itself barely perched above the water.

Morning arrived, ashamed of itself. Three more had died during the night.

Kemp was on board the Talma when Henry Nowabbi came beside him.

"They're dawdling," Henry said. "Giving him time."

John Crabb, another agent, scoffed at that. "There's no way that Indian makes it back," he said. "The way the river's icing, we don't go now, we won't make it either."

Kemp looked out at the Choctaws. Time, this deadline for leaving, was bearing down on them. "Tell them to get on board or they'll be left behind," he said.

The agents, desperate to be away, soon had the entire company crowded on board.

"There's no sign of stragglers," Sonny Istubby said, though Kemp hadn't asked. "Still, was it me, I'd wait a bit."

"Another half hour, we'll be iced in, Kemp," Crabb said. "No provisions, the cholera on its way—we wait, it's a death sentence for all."

Kemp looked at the sky, the river, the Choctaws on board, then turned to Crabb. "Tell the captain to get under way," he said. "Now."

Anoni had helped her cousin pull herself to the stern of the boat, but there was nothing to see but those two foes that had done them so much damage already, water and ice. She had no realistic hope to keep her there, only foolish hope. As the boat's mates made ready and the bell rang out, her heart jumped at something in the distance; but it was only a log come bobbing up in the water. Tired beyond endurance, she sank to the deck. There was no hope after all, even foolish. The boat was pulling away. Time had won.

Kemp was forward in the boat when the cry went up. He pushed his way through the crowd and looked east. There, running through the waist-high water where the river had overflowed its banks, knees pumping high, water churning right and left, was Wild-at-Heart, straining to reach the boat before it was too late. And he carried something in his arms.

Wild-at-Heart wore no shirt, no coat. What was left of his shirt was wrapped around the bundle in his arms. His face was red and distorted, his muscles bulged grotesquely and his frozen fingers barely held their grip on his burden. He came on, relentless and methodical, pounding his way through the muddy water that reached up to his waist, grabbing at him, slowing him down, pulling him back, until finally, with a ferocious surge, he abandoned the water and gained the wooden ramp leading to the boat, now slowly drifting away. The Choctaws onboard howled for the boat to stop but knew it would not. And then they saw that Wild-at-Heart would not make it. The distance between the boat and dock already was too great. Even this close, he and the girl would be left behind—to the ice, the exposure, the cholera. Death would have him sooner rather than later. And then, in one of those moments that will always be told, the Choctaw brave hit the end of the dock running. He did not hesitate, he did not slow. It never occurred to him not to try. He jumped. It was an impossible distance to clear.

The story of the Choctaw brave going back to rescue the child would be told again and again down through the years. The distance that Wild-at-Heart jumped from the shore to the boat grew further and further with each retelling.

Finally, they said he flew.

Wild-at-Heart fell into the throng of outstretched hands, clutching the little girl. She was pale, wet, insensible and half-frozen…but still alive. She was carried off to be tended to while Wild-at-Heart lay on the deck. He was staring at the sky and even under such duress he wore his foolish, lopsided grin.

Later, they learned he had run all night.

The captain guided the boat farther into the river's channel and on its way. Kemp had watched the wild run for the boat, the leap, the cheering throng, without a word. Now he moved back to the bow and looked out at the grey morning. He couldn't have said what he was feeling. He was simply glad to be away.

There was still a long way to go.

The Talma steamed up the Ouachita River to Écore à Fabre in Arkansas and unloaded the final party to join the Choctaws already there. Those eleven hundred weary souls set out across treacherous roads and impenetrable swamps the remaining one hundred and sixty-five miles to the new Indian territory. More of them died. At last, early in March 1832, five months after they started, they reached Fort Towson. They were, for want of a better word, home.

Wild-at-Heart spent three weeks putting up a house that would serve for his mother at a spot she favored. The day he finished he walked into town to a store at the end of the main street, picked out what he needed, paid for it and said he would get it Monday next, the day that had been arranged with the Light Horse.

The evening before he was to go into town, Wild-at-Heart sat with his mother. "I'm going to have me a little stew," she said, and he ate with her. "It seems like my head kindly wants to hurt," she said later. Wild-at-Heart liked to listen to her. He liked her voice.

At dusk, Dolphie Gardner made his way to the house and asked for Wild-at-Heart. The young man came out and the two sat for an hour and never said a word, as was their way. At the end of the hour, Dolphie arose and went on his way. Wild-at-Heart was glad he had come.

Will Kemp, who had stayed on in the area though he couldn't have said why, passed that way that night. He sat his horse high on a hill overlooking Anoni's place. He watched the old man come and go. He thought about his home back in Mississippi. It seemed much further than five hundred miles away; it seemed thousands and thousands of miles behind. It seemed impossible for a man to ride in that direction, as if some kind of natural law had been passed that prevented it; all the world now had to go west. He felt he would have had to go all the way around the globe to make it back there. He thought about a girl from there. He barely knew her. Once she sang a haunting song and he thought about talking to her, but had not. He wondered if he would be lonesome all his life.

The day set for the execution arrived and found a small crowd of settlers gathered to witness the proceedings. As the hour for the execution drew nearer with no sign of Wild-at-Heart, some began to grumble, feeling they might be cheated out of something, while others guffawed and made wagers on whether the foolish fellow would show at all. Will Kemp was there standing off from the rowdy group.

One loud, curly-haired youth named Calvin had great sport calling out the time whenever ten minutes or so had passed and the time set for the show drew nearer with no sign of the main character. The boy talked on any and all matters, proclaiming at one time how dastardly the condemned man would be if he didn't show and at another how foolish he would be if he did.

"Did I tell you boys," he called on one occasion, "that I caught a jackrabbit yesterday? Being as I'd already eaten, I told him I'd turn him loose if he'd agree to show up here today and let me skin him and eat him then. Well, he was amenable to the suggestion and swore on his life he'd be here. But you know what, boys? It's getting late and I haven't seen hide nor hair of that jack yet!"

The other lads roared with him. This was great sport, and no one thought of the consequences.

As more people arrived to witness the scene, Calvin repeated his story of the untrustworthy rabbit, and more bets were placed on Wild-at-Heart than on a horse race, when the outcome there was only who crossed the finish line first.

As for the little company of Choctaws sitting on the ground heedless to any of the goings-on, it never entered their heads to wonder if Wild-at-Heart would show.

The minutes melted away. A late afternoon thunderstorm came up, sudden and sad, but before anyone outside could get in, before anyone inside could get to the window to see, it was already past, already moving on. All anyone saw was its back and the late evening, yellow glow of the sun returned. They watched it go, leaving them behind, and they were wistful. And when they turned back from looking, Wild-at-Heart was there. True to his word, he had come for his own execution and we can only wonder what thoughts passed through his mind on that trip into town. He approached the company of Choctaws and sat down.

The chatter and noise from the settlers came to a halt. If bets actually had been made there was nothing to show it; no money exchanged hands, no one whooped and hollered. And, to their credit, no one felt he had won anything.

Will Kemp pushed himself back from the rail he had been leaning on, caught his horse's reins and pulled himself into the saddle. He had seen enough. All his life had been lived in Mississippi. But he would not go back there. He would head west, toward the prairie, toward the places that still had few people and no names, places whose stories had not yet been written. He turned now to the big blond youth called Calvin.

"You know that rabbit you've been going on about, fellow?" he said in a husky voice, and Calvin nodded. "It must not have been Choctaw."

As he rode away, he was vaguely aware that he was proud of something. He just couldn't have said what.

Wild-at-Heart sat among the circle of Choctaws. Those who knew him took turns shaking his hand, saying their farewells. To each Wild-at-Heart listened but did not himself speak; the good fellow did not want to say anything foolish. The Light Horseman, Henry Nowabbi, asked if there was anything he needed but Wild-at-Heart said no. Henry said there was food for him if he wanted but Wild-at-Heart said he had had a little cornbread earlier and that would do him. His mother came forward and slowly and calmly combed his long, black hair while her heart broke.

Too quickly, the time was gone and, without prodding, Wild-at-Heart walked to the appointed place where he stood in front of the coffin he had picked out and paid for two days earlier. Henry opened the condemned man's shirt and daubed a spot of red paint above the heart while Wild-at-Heart watched. He apologized sheepishly for being so much trouble. He took a moment and then said that he was ready. Henry tied a blindfold around his eyes and straightway signaled for a man, hidden until now, to come forward. It was Sonny Istubby and it was he—the boy who had thrown a piece of hard candy— Wild-at-Heart had asked to perform the execution. Sonny came forward, placed the rifle muzzle against his friend's chest and fired.

The crack of the rifle was very small for what it had done. Wild-at-Heart fell. And something was lost and something was gained.

Henry and Sonny helped Wild-at-Heart's mother, who had given him that name, place her son's body in the coffin and then into the grave he had dug for himself. The affair had come to a close.

After everyone else had left, a lad of seven or eight crawled out from under a wagon where he had hidden to watch. So strong were his feelings it would be hard to say what they were. He sobbed. He yelled. He laughed. He felt as if he must do something. Save someone. Fight someone. Run through the woods growling like a bear. Jump all the way to the moon. Shoot a bow and arrow further than anyone ever had shot one before. Something.

He couldn't do any of those things.

He had no bow, no arrow, no weapon. He had no field, no land, no office, no title, no rank, no power, no privilege. All he had was a story to tell, and that story was unstoppable.

The place was empty now save for the sun and it had places to be itself and so can be excused for not lingering. But before it left, contrary to all the laws of nature, it shone just a little brighter on that certain spot. Then it went on, and the boy with it.

And somewhere, William Wallace smiled.

AUTHOR'S NOTE

Much of the background information for this story is drawn from Muriel H. Wright's "The Removal of the Choctaws to the Indian Territory 1830-1833" in *Chronicles of Oklahoma*, June 1928; H.B. Cushman's *History of the Choctaw, Chickasaw and Natchez Indians*; and accounts of Choctaw justice in various newspapers, including the *Muscogee Indian Journal*.

––––––––––––

James Masters has been writing fiction and non-fiction for more than 30 years. He has a Ph.D in drama and worked in the theater in New York for five years. He is a member of the Choctaw Nation of Oklahoma and lives in Shawnee, Oklahoma.

––––––––––––

TOWARD THE SETTING SUN

Ramona Choate Schrader

"Not all walked with their heads down."—Olin Williams, Cultural Preservation Specialist, Choctaw Nation of Oklahoma.

When the time of the Removal came, it did not begin in tragedy for all. Some were in a better situation as they prepared for the long journey. But no amount of preparation guarantees the security of a family.

Sometimes, all you can do is continue on toward the setting sun.

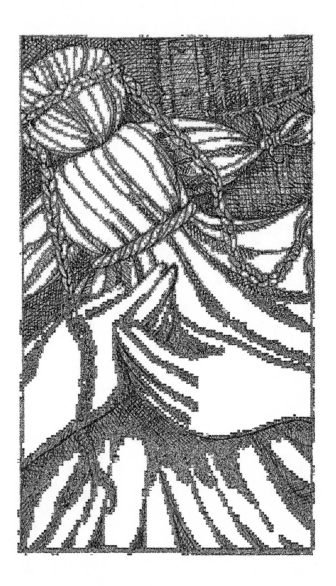

Toward the Setting Sun

Ramona Choate Schrader

I have read that studies suggest we are all born with genetic memories; that we move through time carrying the experiences and culture of our ancestors.

No wonder I felt the pain and suffering of the Choctaws as I wrote this story. It was as though I was there, on the trail with my tribe during this historic struggle.

This story begins in a quiet country community near central Mississippi. Neat houses of logs with wide porches and native stone fireplaces were the homes of Native Americans known as the Choctaw tribe.

The large house near the creek, with its beautiful shade trees, belonged to the Hardsaw family. Jess was head of the family, a hardworking and successful farmer and cattle breeder. Long before, his father had purchased a bull and two heifers from a French Canadian who settled near the Choctaws. The man helped them accept cattle breeding as an adjunct to farming. It proved popular since abundant wild game was gone forever, and the Choctaws loved red meat.

Women held a special place in the Choctaw family. Martha, Jess' wife, offered wisdom and hope in all situations her family faced. She knew how to prepare good meals, and how to prepare for any trouble that came.

Together, Jess and Martha had three children. The oldest, Tim, was twelve. He was a good hunter and brought the game to his mother for her to cook. Calvin was his nine-year-old brother. They spent long hours each day either working or playing. Some months they attended the Mission School. Education was important to the Choctaw tribe. They supported the schools when they received payments from the United States government for lands that were traded in the treaties.

Tim was big for his age and strong. He was a leader at school and good in his studies. Often when Jess had to be away taking crops or cattle to market, he could depend on Tim to take over the farm and care for the animals.

The third child in the Hardsaw family was six-year-old Lydia. She was small, frail, but fun and pretty. She had just started Mission School and was already reading some.

Lydia mainly stayed near the house but sometimes she ventured out to the creek with Tim and Calvin. The boys played in the water and hunted for crawfish, but she looked for colorful rocks and gathered wildflowers. She often found arrowheads left over from hunters.

They knew where the wild berries grew, and when they ripened, the children picked enough for their mother to make a cobbler. Grape dumplings were popular and family recipes were handed down to the new brides.

One day, Lydia called the boys to where she was standing near the creek bank. She pointed to the grass. "Look," she said.

"Baby rabbits! Where is their mother?"

Tim and Calvin ran to her, and Tim said, "Their mother is searching for food. She will be back. Don't touch them." So they just looked at the baby animals.

The children checked on the rabbits for a few days. The next time they ran to the creek bank, the bunnies were gone. Lydia looked alarmed but Tim said, "Don't worry, they had grown enough to hop away with their mother."

This calmed Lydia, and she smiled.

One afternoon, Tim came running into the kitchen carrying a string of fish. Martha was baking pies and she looked up with a big smile on her face. She was beautiful with high cheekbones, black hair and smooth skin. She had folded her hair to the center back of her head then tied the middle of the folds with a cloth ribbon in a bow as many Choctaw women did.

"*Yakoke*, Tim, for the supper." She gazed at him. "I appreciate the things you do for the family. You help me so much with the younger children."

The praise sending a pleasing flutter through him, Tim sat down on the willow and cane stool nearby. "Mother, I heard from some boys that we have to leave our homes here and go west of the Mississippi River many miles. Is that true?"

The oven was hot now so Martha put the pies in. "Let's go out on the porch and have a glass of peppermint tea." Made with water from the nearby spring and fresh mint sprigs, it was cool and delicious. Tim loved sitting in the willow rockers and talking with his mother.

He knew from the worried look on her face this was not an easy conversation for her. "It is true what you heard, but your father and I wanted to wait a while longer before we told you and the others."

Tim sat still, waiting as his mother tried to form a way to explain the situation in simple terms for him.

She said, "There have been many treaties with the government and many promises were never kept. Now the treaty at Dancing Rabbit Creek has been signed by our tribal leaders. They really had no choice. President Jackson told the Choctaws they must move or perish. We are being forced even though we were told the decision would be ours."

Tim frowned. This had been the Choctaw homeland for hundreds of years. They were leaving their sacred burial mound, *Nanih Waiya*. It was hard to think about it all.

"Tim," his mother said with sadness in her voice, "you will remember our home here and our trips to the ancestral burial ground."

"Yes, Mother, this will always be a special place to me. Our families have lived here for generations. I will not forget."

He thought about the creeks, the woods, and his pony. He loved riding to Mission School where he enjoyed being with the other children. He couldn't imagine what the new country would be like. It was rumored to be a wilderness and his people faced hard work. But he felt it would be well because his parents were strong people and had the desire to be happy and successful. And they had faith.

"Mother, we can do it; we won't be alone," he said. "God will go with us."

Martha smiled and nodded, then reassured him all his friends and their families would go, too. She explained that because thousands would move they could not all travel together, and how in her heart she knew the journey would be difficult. It was over five hundred miles and she had heard there would be wide rivers, trails over rough ground, swamps and some mountains. There would be few roads.

She jumped up to finish the evening meal, and told Tim to start his chores. Always hopeful, she added, "Let's look at the removal as a great adventure."

Tim and his brother helped feed the livestock and bring in firewood. He loved helping his father with any job on the farm. How he would miss this place!

As he and Calvin began chores, his little sister, Lydia, asked to help. He put some dried corn in a little bucket and said, "You can feed the chickens with me. See if there are any eggs in their nests. Let me know and I will help you gather them."

Lydia smiled, happy to help. She held her most treasured possession—a cornhusk doll—in one hand as she worked. "Tim, why are we going away?"

Startled, Tim realized Lydia must have heard the same rumors. He tried to think of how to explain to his little sister what he did not fully comprehend himself. "The grown-ups argued it a long time. For some reason, it seems best we leave for a new land."

"Oh," Lydia said as though she understood. She took a tiny handful of corn and spread it around for the excited chickens.

Tim continued, "It'll be a grand adventure. We will see things we never have before."

Lydia paused from her task to straighten the silky braids of her doll.

"You can ride on my pony while we travel." Tim held the egg basket low while Lydia carefully added one to it.

Lydia nodded in her good way as they finished gathering

eggs and she stroked her doll's braids.

Tim wondered how she would be able to travel to the new country. She was not a strong child and even had trouble walking sometimes. She tired easily and she ate little. He would tease her and say, "You eat like a tiny bird!"

He loved his sister and knew in his heart he had to help her all he could on the journey.

That evening the family gathered around the table and had a blessing. His father prayed that God would be with them on the upcoming trip.

As they ate their meal in front of the window, Tim glanced up and saw the glow of the sun. "Look there, toward the west and see the sunset over the creek. We will be able to see that same sunset in our new home."

Martha was touched by this and said, "Yes, Tim, as we travel west toward our new home, we will see that same sunset each evening if the weather is good. It will be a welcome sight and a reminder of our home here and our future there in the new land. Let's remember this."

The children were in their beds up in the loft overlooking the living room. Martha and Jess sat in their chairs and talked about the Removal. Nothing like it had been done before.

Martha had questions of her own and she wanted Jess to give her reassurance and some answers. He had been attending tribal meetings concerning the treaty and the Removal.

Jess said, "You remember since the treaty of 1803, there has been talk of our removal as a tribe to another land to the west, so the white man can live here."

Though she had been young, Martha recalled that time, but since then her people had made great strides in their development. They had established more schools and accepted the Christian faith. They intermarried with the European settlers and became successful farmers. They even had a constitutional government.

"Now with the signing of the Treaty of Dancing Rabbit Creek, we must move." Jess spoke with sadness in his voice.

Martha folded her hands together to keep them from trembling. She whispered, "What about the children? Little Lydia is so small and frail. The boys are still young. Must they suffer so? How could our leaders sign such a treaty?"

Jess looked at her with understanding in his eyes. "It will be hard, but we can do it because we have each other and our faith. We must be strong for the children."

As the summer waned into fall, Martha and Jess talked about the plans for the removal of the Choctaws. Jess attended the meetings and reported to Martha as things progressed.

Finally, he announced that the U.S. government had set October 1831 for the first group of people to leave and after that, two more groups in the coming years. The first group would be about four thousand people. By then, even the children knew that the land where they were going was to be Indian territory.

The official in charge told the Hardsaw family that because they were located in the northern part of their present country, they needed to go to Memphis and join the group they would travel with. The people who lived in the southern part of Mississippi would meet in Vicksburg.

It seemed well-planned in the beginning. The government officials told them they wanted this journey to be as trouble-free as possible. It seemed it would be to Tim and his family.

But as the time approached, the weather turned. With heavy rain, the roads flooded and became almost impassible. Still the government officials in charge were determined to start.

Now the looming question for Martha as she made preparations, was what possessions they should take. The ones in charge said they should leave everything and be reimbursed in Indian Territory. She could not do this. Some of her belongings had been her mother's and even her grandmother's. They could not be replaced. She had to take as much as possible of the family things that meant so much. But what could stand the rough journey?

Jess bought a wagon so he could outfit it his own way. The people were told they would be reimbursed and given the proper tools to build houses and plant crops when they arrived in Indian Territory, but he still wanted to be prepared himself.

Martha heard from a neighbor that white people were already trying to move into the farms even before the Choctaws could move out. One neighbor reported livestock missing. It was clear the white people were eager to take over their land.

Jess had talked to a white family about buying his place and some of his equipment. He wouldn't get the money now as the title work had to be done. All of this was in the hands of the U.S. government and it would take time. He knew they may never get the money.

Finally, the last item was loaded into the wagon. Tim tucked in a couple of his books and silently hoped they would make it. One was a book of poems. Calvin made sure the stickball equipment was put in a safe place for the journey. The brothers asked Lydia if she had her cornhusk doll. They were ready for their adventure.

The first week of October 1831, the long journey began.

As they left, the women formed a long line into the woods and walked among the old trees, stroking their leaves and, with bowed heads, gave an unspoken farewell. It was a heartrending day for the tribe.

Some families were provided a wagon but those who weren't, walked. Some rode horses. All left in silence with heavy hearts.

They had rough going from the start because of the heavy rains. They camped at night and cooked their meals as best they could. Martha was thankful she had enough provisions for a few weeks because the amount of food the government handed out was not nearly enough to sustain them.

At first, the children thought it was a real adventure. Tim was excited when he learned part of the journey would be on a riverboat and ferries into Arkansas. But soon, even the little ones realized it was slow-going and harder each day.

On a good day, the group traveled fifteen miles. Martha hoped the weather would improve. It was almost more than the elderly could endure.

Many times there were no roads as they progressed toward Memphis. Freezing temperatures and snow added to their misery. The government agents did not have enough blankets. The clothing the people started out in was not suitable for the conditions. Children had no shoes.

Martha had prepared as much as she could for her family. At least they had some heavy clothes and boots for their feet.

She tried to shield her children from the suffering around them.

Older people were dying and the travelers stopped along the way for proper burial. The suffering increased daily. They finally arrived in Memphis and were told the riverboats weren't ready.

The Choctaws made camp and discovered a lack of tents. Many slept out in the elements. Food was scarce. Even the livestock was starving.

A witness in Memphis told of the tragedy of the Choctaws. He wrote "…the band of Indians traveled through the town in complete silence. Not a sound was heard as they slashed along through the icy weather."

A Choctaw chief expressed his feelings of the ordeal: "A trail of tears and death."

Tim and his little brother found there was not time for games. They did enjoy the short riverboat ride but soon they were back on land headed toward Little Rock. Part of the time, Tim drove the oxen that pulled the wagon.

After days on their journey, the children were hungry most of the time. The group that Tim and his family were traveling with missed some of the swamps but later they heard how terrible that route had been. The horses mired in the mud and were too weak to pull themselves out. There were half as many horses now as there had been at the beginning.

Tim asked his mother how the family provisions were holding out. He had noticed how worried she looked, especially when Lydia was nearby. He knew his sister was tired most of the time. His mother kept her in their wagon, and at camp in the evenings she kept her away from other people. Lydia had little resistance now.

So many had contracted cholera and the Choctaws were dying at an alarming rate. The people had not realized at the time that the disease had come down the Mississippi River on the boats.

The government agents found it difficult to purchase food from local farmers. The farmers asked double the normal fee. The people were given a handful of corn, one turnip and a few cups of water each day. Sometimes they were given meat, but much of it was spoiled. It was hardly enough to sustain a person. Martha and Jess tried to keep a cheerful attitude and each night the family ate their rations together near the campfire. If it was raining, they huddled in their covered wagon. The parents watched Lydia getting weaker.

Some of the farmers along the trail took pity on the Choctaws. One family offered them pumpkins from a small patch. Most were so hungry they ate the pumpkin raw. Another farmer offered them winter turnips. None of the Indians took food without permission. And the fact they didn't beg made an impression on the white people.

It became apparent Lydia needed medicine, but there was no doctor on the trail. Martha didn't know what it was since the tribe had come in contact with several diseases. All she could do was try to keep her warm and feed her small amounts of food and hot broth. But she didn't improve.

On a clear day, the brothers hunted for rabbits but so did others in the traveling party. Game was scarce.

The sickness kept them moving at a slow march. But they kept going. The old and the sick and the young walked as long as they could. If they stopped, they died.

Conditions worsened and typhoid broke out. At one point, thirteen wagons were filled with sick Choctaws. Each afternoon they camped so they could get food rations and wait for the slower ones to catch up. The dead were buried in shallow graves because of the frozen ground.

One morning Martha woke with Lydia in her arms, the tiny girl barely breathing. Her little breath was shallow and her eyes half-closed. Martha called Jess and they quietly discussed telling the boys Lydia was slipping fast.

When they brought the boys together, they told them their little sister was dying. Martha brushed the back of her fingers across the forehead of her unconscious daughter. "She is suffering. If God chooses to take her, He knows best. We know that she will be in a happy place and someday we will all see her again."

As little Lydia took a final breath, they realized they had suffered like the others; they had lost a loved one.

The boys watched with tears in their eyes as Lydia's tiny body was wrapped in her blanket and laid in a shallow grave. Tim sniffed back his tears. "Mama, put her cornhusk doll in with her. She would like that."

In her grief, Martha had not thought of that. "Thank you, Tim, for remembering," she said, tears streaming down her face.

The doll was one her grandmother had made for her. Lydia had treasured and took great care of it, even on the trail and through her sickness. The doll's silky braids were made from a horse's mane.

Several others were buried along with Lydia. The people

sang and there were prayers and the tears flowed. Tim and Calvin promised to never forget their sister and her bravery. They would have sweet memories forever.

Tim had written a poem on his slate board and read it aloud.

Little sister, the wildflowers bloom
where you once played,
The sun still shines on green grass blades,
Above, the wind whispers softly in the trees,
Go gently.

Let your spirit soar in the breeze
And we will one day meet again
Where moonbeams dance and angels sing,
Go gently.

After the burial, the little Choctaw family was more determined to make it to the new land. But the march continued. One of the leaders of the Removal said of the Choctaws: "They are a people that will walk to the last, or I do not know how we could go on."

The people felt they were approaching Indian Territory. Their numbers had dwindled by the hundreds, but the look on the travelers' faces was of hope and great determination. They had traversed over five hundred miles. It had been a torturous journey and no family was spared suffering.

As the boys walked beside the wagon that carried their mother, they notice how much thinner and older she looked. They knew she was mourning the loss of their little sister.

It had been five months since the beginning of the courageous journey, the end of the first official Removal of the Choctaws from their ancestral home in Mississippi. As the Choctaws entered their new territory, those who had arrived earlier rushed to meet them. There was much jubilation, yet grief.

Martha embraced friends and family members. *Not all tears are of sadness. Sometimes there are tears of joy.* She looked over the hills and prairie and thought the land was beautiful. *Yes, we can be happy here. May we never have to move again*, she prayed.

Her thoughts went to their great loss, Lydia, their baby. She looked around at the families nearby and knew others were feeling the same emotion. There had been so much heartache.

Then she gazed toward the setting sun, the western horizon. It was billowing in brilliant shades of red and orange. How lovely to her tired eyes. She glanced over to where Tim was standing. He was looking in the same direction and experiencing the almost spiritual sight. It was surreal. Tim walked over to his mother and held her hand. "Mother, this is God's sign of hope!"

And it was. Their journey was over, and their future would begin with a new sunrise.

Daughter of an original Dawes enrollee, **Ramona Choate Schrader** has been a proud member of the Choctaw Nation of Oklahoma all her life. She was born on the family farm at Choate Prairie, Indianola, Oklahoma, in the house built by her great-grandfather on his original allotment land. It is now on the National Historic Register.

George Washington Choate, her great-grandfather, was the last president of the Choctaw Senate. He was thirteen at the time of the Removal.

Ms. Schrader writes by hand where she resides in Knoxville, Tennessee, near family, though she makes frequent trips west to reconnect with her Oklahoma roots.

OKCHAKKO: A COLT'S JOURNEY

Francine Locke Bray

Before Removal, the U.S government planned to take all the livestock at a value of "some discreet person." In actuality, the Choctaws had trouble getting a fair price for their cattle, horses, and other animals. They also knew the need for starter stock in the new land, and doubted the government's promise of reimbursement. When Removal began, the Choctaws did not leave all their valuable livestock behind.

Thousands of horses experienced their own trail of tears. This is the tale of one.

Okchakko: A Colt's Journey

Francine Locke Bray

My name is Okchakko; that is what the humans call me. I heard them say I am about fourteen and a half hands high from ground to withers, have a white blaze on my face and white socks on my two hind feet, and am a shade of grey with white speckles. In their language, Okchakko means I am Blue.

Listen, for I have an important story to share with you. My humans are a proud native people called *Chahta*. I was born in the spring, sometime shortly before my Chahta had to move from their homes in a place called Mississippi to a land far away to the west. They say that now makes me about thirty in human years. I know only that I am respected as one of the elders of my herd. It is important you listen to the story I am about to tell you. There are not many of us left who made the journey. I think of it as one of the most important events in not only my life but also the lives of my Chahta humans and all their ponies.

My human, a Chahta named Chan, lived in a two-story stone house with his family. I lived in a large pasture surrounded by a five-foot-high fence made of logs. The fence kept me and the rest of the horses from wandering off. My mama, Ohoyo Taha, and papa, Akana Nakni Ola, seemed to be special horses to Chan and his family. We never left this pasture other than with our humans.

Chan owned what was called a stand. He was responsible for finding and collecting stray horses. He tried to find their humans and, if not, the horses either stayed and joined our herd or went with the humans who came by the stand. Humans traveling from one place to another stopped at his stand to eat and sometimes sleep. There was a bunch of horse trading going on. I would buddy up with another colt and then, all of a sudden, he was gone!

Sometime before I was born, humans from far away came and asked my Chahta people to sign a paper that gave their land away to some white-skinned humans called the Americans. My Chahta had to move away to make more room for these humans. According to Chan, they were supposed to sell us and their cattle and oxen but they couldn't so they took us with them on this journey. We didn't know where we were going or how long it would take. But I heard there was a white human they called Lieutenant Jefferson Van Horne who was going to lead us part of the way.

At the time we had to move, I was only six months old and still needed my mama's milk.

All the mares and stallions were snorting, stomping their feet and shaking their heads—acting as if something was very, very wrong. The other foals were also confused, going from gathering in small groups to clinging to their mamas' sides. My mama kept a close eye on me and didn't let me wander far from her. Not only the animals were upset but also the humans. Chan, his family and their helpers were taking the older horses and stallions and putting packs on their backs, sometimes as many as five packs loaded with the things that humans used and valued.

Chaos was everywhere. The humans were rushing around, crying, calling, and yelling to each other and the animals.

"Where are the children?"

"Why do we have to leave?"

"How will we survive?"

My papa, Akana Nakni Ola, was a black stallion and the leader of our herd. Throughout the days of preparation he gathered us into circles, trying to keep his mares and foals together. If he or our mamas saw we were wandering off, they quickly ran to us, ears down, and nipped us—sometimes not gently—on the side. That was our signal to return to the herd and stay close.

"Why are the horses all being confined and some loaded with packs?" I asked Mama. "Why are the oxen being yoked to the wagons? What is happening?"

I was frightened and couldn't figure it all out and Mama didn't seem to have any answers to my questions.

After days of preparation and confusion, we were ready to begin the journey. I heard something about it being November 2, 1832. Whatever that meant. I also heard our group was going to be split up. It was quite large, consisting of Chief Greenwood LeFlore's Chahta. I don't know who decided, but the majority of the Chahta people were to go by water while we—the horses, oxen and cattle—and some of the people were to go overland. Our group included Lt. Van Horne, several families, and several hundred horses. We were quite a large group and everyone wanted to go in different directions. We had some family captains with us, including my Chan, who helped keep us moving in the right direction. Many of the people walked, but some were able to ride in wagons or on our backs.

Lt. Van Horne met us at a place called Vicksburg, Mississippi. He was going to lead us part of the way to a place called Little Rock, Arkansas, where we were to join a larger group of Chahta for the rest of our journey. I had no idea what was ahead of us but, despite being a little frightened by all the changes, I was excited to see new pastures. Little did I know each day would bring adventure, challenge, and tragedy.

The first day we walked eight miles along the bank of a big water—they said it was the Mississippi River—to a place the humans called Thompson's Ferry. There a snag boat, the Heliopolis, began carrying everyone, including us animals, across the river. Our group included Lt. Van Horne, several families of different colors, and two hundred and forty-five horses. We made the crossing without mishap. This was my first time to ride on a boat and I was thrilled. But the boat rocked and sickness washed over me. My legs were real wobbly when I got off the boat. By now I realized I definitely needed to stay very close to my mama. That evening a light rain began but we were able to find a spot for the night near wood, water and a cane brake. That was a good spot.

Lt. Van Horne said we traveled between six and thirty miles every day. The weather, condition of the roads, and whether someone fell behind dictated how many miles we covered. Most of the travel was by bad roads and swamps. After only a couple of days' travel, everyone was tired. I really didn't mind traveling, walking. But I didn't like having to keep moving and not being able to stop, graze and look around.

As each day passed, I did not know what to think. We walked and walked and walked. Sometimes the roads were good, but it rained almost every day and was cold. The availability of cane brakes and forage was never certain and there was no stopping to graze. The humans constantly urged us onward. Occasionally Lt. Van Horne had to purchase fodder for us and the cattle and oxen. One day we traveled twelve miles through a deep and nasty swamp. By then many of us ponies were weak, exhausted and became bogged down. Our hooves would get stuck in the deep mud making it hard to move. I watched in fear and horror as those who could not be pulled out of the swamp were knocked on the head by their humans. I was terrified I would not be able to get out of the swamp. When Mama and I made it to the other side, I ran around and bucked for joy. She quickly nipped me to get me back in line.

When crossing water the humans crossed on rafts or boats, while we—the horses, cattle and oxen—had to swim. The water was cold and dark so we tried to cross as fast as we could. Because of the mud on the banks, we slipped and slid trying to climb out.

Always tired and hungry, I just wanted to stop. Fearing I would not be able to catch up with the group or would get lost, Mama kept nudging me on with either a nip or a shove. One night in particular, I heard that twenty horses wandered off and some of them were never found. We had to move on without them.

The weather did not improve. Sleet added to the rain. One day I heard a Chahta say it was the 8th of November. We traveled only ten miles and had to swim the first of a number of bayous. Lt. Van Horne commented, "The road this day was very bad and weather disagreeable."

Late that night, Lt. Van Horne sat in his tent, writing in his journal. It had been the roughest few days he had ever experienced on this long journey west.

He wrote:

For the last couple of days, I have not been in good health. I am experiencing a severe attack of bilious fever, and my bowels are in a disordered state. For the last day or two I had the dysentery very severely. I had become prostrated. Another soldier of my party came to me this evening and told me that he, too, was sick and believed it was the cholera. He wanted some medicine, which I gave him.

Van Horne sighed, rubbing his eyes to clear them, determined to write his nightly entry as always. In the wilderness and needing a guide, he had hired a man by the name of Morris.

The two of us went to Mr. Morris's house to sleep on the floor. However, we both became so sick, vomiting through the floor boards that Morris told us we had to leave. He was afraid of us infecting his large family, saying their lives were at stake.

We begged him to let us stay. He would not.

Pausing a moment to let his dizziness pass, Van Horne continued.

The ground is covered with frost and it was freezing severely. I rolled myself in my blanket and walked three fourths of a mile to my tent.

A second dose of medicine stayed in his stomach, and by morning he felt relieved. But the opium he took left him dizzy and weak.

On the morning of the 9th, Morris refused to guide the group, fearing the sickness might spread through his large family.

Still weak, Lt. Van Horne mounted his horse before sunrise

and tried to find another guide. The only one he could locate was a young man whom he dismissed upon reaching the Bayou Mason. The youngster simply could not find the right way.

Lt. Van Horne wrote in his journal that evening; *I have not recovered and my suffering for two or three days exceeded anything I ever experienced.*

It was difficult to stay upon his horse and he often dismounted and lay on the ground. Over the next three days the party did cover about thirty-five miles, always traveling through *bad swamp…cane brakes and thick undergrowth…without any road or trail* as well as through yet another swamp. Lt. Van Horne and his fellow soldier did recover from the cholera and were the only two people on the journey to get sick.

I knew that Lt. Van Horne and another man were very sick. Everyone was worried they would not get better and we would have to find our own way. But one night, we were able to camp where there was a lot of cane, wood and good water. This raised everyone's spirits. Lt. Van Horne seemed to be recovering from his sickness. My Chahta family talked about how brave he was—he did not give up but continued to lead us on our journey.

Over the next four days we swam the Bayou Mason, passed Lakeport, crossed the outlet of Old River Lake, traveled through another swamp, and crossed many more bayous. I lost count. We swam while the people had to scramble across on fallen trees. On another day, for about five miles, we passed through cane brakes and thick undergrowth. It was difficult traveling and did not ease up as we then had to travel through eight miles of swamp between the Mississippi River and Bayou

Bartholomew. I thought the swamp was endless and we would never find solid ground again.

At the end of that day Lt. Van Horne again found healthy cane, water and wood which made for good camping and forage. We were hungry, exhausted, wet and cold. I think we all, including the humans, wanted to return to our homes and not travel any further.

The long walk did not get easier. We had to cross yet another bayou, Bayou Bartholomew. The weather was cold so the Chahta people and their belongings crossed in a boat; we, the horses and other animals, again swam. But tasty corn was issued to us that night.

As days went on, I was getting wearier and wearier but Mama prodded me along, encouraging me to keep up. "Keep moving," she said. "You don't want to fall behind. If you do, you will be lost to us."

Then tragedy struck. I experienced the worst day of my short life! Mama and I were passing a large, old tree when a huge branch, heavy with ice, came crashing down, hitting Mama on the neck. She stumbled and fell to the ground.

"Mama, Mama!" I cried. I tried and tried to get her to get up but it seemed she couldn't work her legs. She raised her head a little and looked at me with sad, pleading eyes but she could not hold her head up. It dropped back to the frozen ground.

Not yet having encountered death, I didn't understand what had happened. When she didn't move and the other horses and humans came back to check on us, they told me she was what they called dead. I was an orphan, they said, but now being almost seven months old they told me I could survive without Mama and her milk—the milk I thought would always be there for me, especially when we didn't have good forage.

Confused and sad, I wanted to stay where Mama dropped but the humans and other horses tried to urge me on. Thinking Mama would hear me and get up, I frantically ran to and from her side, crying out to her, "Mama, Mama, get up, please get up!"

Finally, with continued prodding from the other horses, especially my papa, Akana Nakni Ola, and my Chahta, Chan, who came back to rescue me, I continued on the journey.

They said that by now we had traveled about one hundred and fifty miles.

As the days wore on, I dragged my feet and many times fell to the end of the line of travelers. Grieving, I was no longer curious and excited about where we might end up. But the other horses and Chan continued to urge me on. Slowly I began to accept the reality that Mama was not going to continue traveling with me and that I had to take care of myself.

On what the humans said was November 22 we arrived at Brummet's on the old Towson road, eight miles west of Little Rock. We had traveled an additional one hundred and twenty-six miles. Lt. Van Horne, the Chahta people, oxen, cattle and horses traveling with me met up with another group. We would travel together for the remainder of the journey, over two hundred and twenty miles. We were all glad when we heard Lt. Van Horne would continue leading us to our new home.

After we rested several days, Lt. Van Horne started us on the remainder of our journey on what the humans said was the 29th of November. This time there were many more Chahta, over six hundred, and horses with us. I was slowly beginning to cope with losing Mama and the new friends helped. I found it quite fun getting to know the foals from the other group.

There were only one or two bullies, older colts who thought they could tell us younger ones what to do. Sometimes, they even tried to keep us from our food by chasing and nipping at us. As tired as we were from walking, we quickly dodged their chase.

Many of the Chahta people were sick when they joined up with our group of travelers. But compared to what we'd been through, the first few days were easy. We traveled mainly by road. Water, wood and forage were available for us when we stopped. On December 3 we once again came to a flowing body of water. I heard them say it was the Ouachita River. We animals forded the river but apparently it was too deep for the humans so Lt. Van Horne got a ferry to take them across.

Now, we had an elder chief, Etotahoma, traveling with us. The Chahta people seemed to respect and love this elder. But every few days, he fell behind and we had to wait for him to catch up. He rode in what they called a cart and it kept breaking down. On the 5th of December, it again broke down. The Chahta captains went to Lt. Van Horne and asked him to wait until Etotahoma's cart could be fixed. I heard that at first Lt. Van Horne wanted to continue on without Etotahoma's cart but the captains were determined this elder not be left behind. Before the cart was fixed, though, we crossed the Caddo. The river was deep but the teams, young men, and horses had to ford it anyway. It was freezing. I shivered. The women, children, and elders were able to cross by boat. After everyone was across, Lt. Van Horne brought Etotahoma's cart up and had it repaired.

Etotahoma's cart continued to break down and cause us to stop and wait for him and his people to catch up. Finally Lt. Van Horne hired a yoke of oxen to bring the broken cart to our campground. Once again, Lt. Van Horne repaired it. He had a new axle made for the cart. This worked. He was now hoping Etotahoma would be able to travel without any more mishap.

I really wasn't surprised by Lt. Van Horne's kindness. After all, he had led us from Vicksburg, Mississippi, and was always looking after our welfare on this long, long trip. If we couldn't find good cane or forage, he tried to purchase corn for us to eat. We needed it. All of us were getting pretty skinny and our ribs and hip bones began to show. I was always hungry!

It was exhausting to continually walk through the mud, which seemed to get deeper and deeper. It was harder and harder to pull my feet out. My legs just didn't seem to want to work. We still had to cross several rivers. The animals usually swam while the humans crossed on boats or rafts. One difference with this part of the trip was food and forage seemed better. Most of our resting sites had good water, wood and forage. This helped keep us from getting too hungry and certainly kept our spirits up.

On what the humans called the 18th of December, many Chahta people came to meet us. They had made the journey before us and apparently came to greet their family members and friends in our group. They were quite a sight to see, all dressed up. Lt. Van Horne seemed impressed with their appearance. We made a final encampment four miles from what they said was Clear Creek. I heard Lt. Van Horne say that 648 Chahta humans completed the trip. I don't remember him saying how many horses, cattle and oxen made it.

Despite the difficulties we encountered and the loss of my mama, I began to feel excitement. I saw pasture and water but there were also what the humans were calling mountains. I was not sure how or where we would live, but I was glad the trip was over. I heard that Lt. Van Horne and the Chahta captains would divide us and we would be taken to our new homes. I wondered where that would be. The farmland, the mountains, the pastures? Where? The next day my Chahta, Chan, decided to head north to an area they called Fort Smith. Others went toward the Kiamichi River and the Red River. We finally stopped traveling just south of Fort Smith, near the Winding Stair Mountains.

Our home is near a place called Howe. We have a creek, lots of pasture, a pond, woods and even cattle. Chan built a two-story house for my Chahta family to live in.

I sometimes think about that long, long walk. For a long time I missed Mama, but when I reached maturity I was able to have some mares of my own and a family. My Chahta, Chan, died several years ago. I expect I will live out the rest of my life with his family here on the farm. Even though we are not in Mississippi, we are home.

AUTHOR'S NOTE

In 1832, Lieutenant Jefferson Van Horne—U.S. Disbursing Agent for the Removal of Indians—was commissioned with the task of escorting two parties of emigrating Choctaws. He kept a report journal of both trips west. Much of this story was based on that journal.

In their new homeland the Chahta people maintained their herds of Chahta ponies. Today, however, they are on the Livestock Conservancy endangered Conservation Priority List (CPL) with less than 250 remaining. The foundation herds, owned by Bryant and Darlene Rickman, are located in Southeastern Oklahoma, near the lands where the horses' ancestors grazed since their removal to Indian Territory.

———

For over 35 years, **Francine Locke Bray** has conducted genealogical and historical research. The past five years she has concentrated primarily on researching the history of the Choctaw horse. Francine has published several articles on the horses, as well as authored educational documents and given oral presentations. She assisted in the research of two historical novels, *Choctaw Kisses, Bullets, and Blood* and *Alice and J.F.B.*, the hundred-year saga of two Seminole chiefs authored by Vance Trimble, and worked with Bettye Broyles on the book, *Locke Family History*.

Francine is a member of the Choctaw Nation of Oklahoma. She and her husband, Michael, live in Antlers, Oklahoma.

———

ONE MISSISSIPPI CLAY BOWL

Leslie Widener

What's important about the journey of one little handmade clay bowl? Perhaps nothing. Perhaps it's the story it tells of the owner's life on her journey of courage, tragedy, and broken pieces. In her shattered world, Nayukpu must keep the pieces of her family together—at least in her heart.

One Mississippi Clay Bowl

Leslie Widener

"Look around and find one thing to write about for your report," Mrs. Fogelman called to the crowded room of seventh-graders. The teacher's voice echoed, bouncing off the walls and exhibit cases in the basement of the art museum.

Savannah grabbed Janie's arm and the girls moved quickly through the group of students to put distance between themselves and their teacher. At the back wall, they leaned against floor-to-ceiling glass cases filled with shelves of red and white painted clay pots. Their noses touched the glass as they stared at the exhibits.

Savannah noticed the cobwebs in the corners of the dingy display case and the dim, narrow room felt cramped. The glass was smudged and she rubbed the spot where her nose had left an imprint. But the exhibit, consisting of hundreds of pieces of pottery, was interesting in spite of a shabby presentation. There were large, round pots with geometric designs painted on the clay in cream and black. Tall urns with two or more handles stood next to low, almost flat ones. Some of the pottery had elaborately painted or carved designs of plants or animals, but others were simple with little decoration, if any. Each had a plaque next to it explaining the original use.

The two girls stayed where they were while Mrs. Fogelman guided the rest of the noisy group out of the pottery room to the next basement exhibit. Over the heads of her classmates, Savannah could see large glass cases filled with ancient, pale-skinned mannequins dressed in ceremonial regalia. Sounds of laughter drifted back toward them.

Mrs. Fogelman raised her voice over the noisy chaos. "Class," she called out. "Remember, this two-page paper equals twenty percent of your semester grade!"

Groans went around the room but the group settled down. The rustle of notebook paper and pens hitting the floor could be heard as students shuffled down the long corridor looking for information to copy.

Pointing to a tall jug with a twisted handle, Janie said, "I like that one." She opened her notebook and began to write.

Savannah wandered further, reading the cards next to each item; "Dough Bowl, Mississippi circa 1850-60," "Effigy Vessel, circa 1750-1800." Nothing caught her eye until she spotted a particular bowl. What set this one apart wasn't its size or beauty, but its homely appearance. It was smaller, about two inches high and twice as wide. The etched design on its darkened surface had nearly disappeared. Though it had been partially repaired, the rim was chipped and a crack ran from the top edge to a large hole in the bottom.

Savannah wondered why this piece had been included in the collection. It sat on a small pedestal, displayed as though it were equally as important as the larger and more decorative pottery. The plaque next to it read; "Eating Bowl, Choctaw, circa 1830s, Pre-Removal."

"Janie, come over here. I think I'll write about this one," she called to her friend, pointing at the bowl. "I wonder what 'pre-removal' means? Removal from where?"

Janie stopped writing long enough to look where Savannah pointed. "Yuck. It's broken. Why would you want to write about that one?"

Savannah flipped to a blank page in her notebook and lifted her chin. "Cause it's Choctaw and so am I." She didn't know much about her Choctaw heritage, but she'd been told her great-grandmother had spoken only the Choctaw language. Now she wished she knew more.

"That's an interesting piece of pottery, for sure," an unfamiliar voice spoke up behind her. "I wish I knew the story behind that little bowl."

Startled, Savannah whirled around and looked up at a tall woman towering over her. Her frizzy blonde hair surrounded her face like a halo and she wore a khaki shirt stitched with the museum's logo. She grinned broadly.

"Hi." She stuck out her hand. "I'm Tara. I'm the one who dug that old thing out of the mud in Arkansas."

Savannah hesitated only for a moment and then reached out to shake hands.

Tara went on. "Did I hear you tell your friend you're Choctaw?"

Savannah nodded shyly at the talkative woman.

"Then who knows, maybe one of your ancestors lost that bowl during their journey from Mississippi to Oklahoma on the Trail of Tears."

"The Trail of Tears," Savannah repeated softly, as she turned back to stare at the broken piece of pottery.

Mississippi, 1830

The clay was warm and moist as they dug it from the banks of the creek bed. Not too sandy or rocky, it was good for making pottery. The wet clay was placed in a woven basket to carry back to the village.

Nayukpu skipped alongside her mother in excitement as they headed home. This was the day she would learn how to make pots like Mother and Grandmother made.

Thwack! The ball of clay hit the rock and flattened. With strong hands, Nayukpu's mother gathered the clay back into a ball and then pushed it away. She repeated this over and over as she kneaded, working out the air until the clay was smooth and firm. Then she broke off a lump and handed it to Nayukpu.

"Now, you try and I will watch you," she said.

Nayukpu practiced over and over to become familiar with the feel of the clay. She was in a hurry to show how she, too, could make a fine pot. But soon, she saw it looked much easier than it actually was.

Her mother and grandmother were masters in the art of making beautiful and useful pottery. Their vessels were traded to other villagers for important things like food, furs and cloth. It was Nayukpu's dream to be just like them, one day.

Grandmother joined them. She sat facing her grand-daughter and placed a walnut-size ball of clay between Nayukpu's hands. She then cupped her hands on either side of

Nayukpu's smaller hands. Together they rolled the clay back and forth as a rope formed. This rope was then coiled around and around to become the base of a pot.

Nayukpu began to form the ropes herself. She built up the sides to form a small round bowl. Mother showed her how to smooth the sides of the bowl with a small wooden paddle. At last, it was complete.

"It's beautiful, daughter! Soon you will be a master potter!"

Nayukpu felt proud as she handed her creation to her grandmother. It was placed on a drying shelf next to the other pots, out of the sun to cure. The pots would dry and designs could be etched on their surfaces before they were baked hard in a fire. Then they would be ready to use for cooking and serving meals.

One Year Later
Mississippi, 1831 Late September

Nayukpu and her family awoke to shouting. They ran out of their small cabin into the morning sunshine and saw soldiers on horseback as they rode through the village, yelling and waving their guns. Screams from frightened women and children filled the air.

Nayukpu saw her uncle coming for her father and the two of them rushed toward the chaos as Mother and Grandmother ran back into the cabin. Nayukpu grabbed her younger brother, Fani, by the hand and followed the women inside.

"What's happening?" Nayukpu cried out.

"Hurry!" Mother thrust a blanket in Nayukpu's arms. "I've heard of them burning down the houses!"

Nayukpu clutched the blanket to her chest as Fani squeezed against her. They watched as the elder women grabbed baskets and filled them with food and cooking items. Her mother laid out a blanket, heaped it with clothing and wrapped it up to be carried out. With haste, her grandmother carefully wound cloth around pieces of pottery and tucked them into a large basket.

"Where are we going?" Nayukpu swallowed a sob and Fani began to cry.

Ignoring her question, her mother shouted, "Don't just stand there! Grab whatever you can. We haven't much time."

Commanded to action, Nayukpu and Fani quickly spread the blanket on the floor. They gathered cups, bowls, a large wooden spoon, dried herbs and a large sack of corn, piling everything in the middle of the blanket. Nayukpu took the corners and tied them together and slung the heavy bag over her shoulder. They scrambled to gather as many precious belongings as they could.

Suddenly, Grandmother startled them by uttering a shrill cry. She pointed to the thatch-covered roof where fingers of black, acrid smoke curled down and began to fill the room. Flames crackled directly over their heads.

With the heavy bundle on her back, Nayukpu grabbed Fani's hand and pulled him out of the cabin. Mother and Grandmother followed. Together, they ran to the edge of the woods surrounding their small village and stood with friends and family. Nayukpu knew, with an ache in her heart, the future of the Homma clan had changed. Men, women and children watched helplessly as the entire village, the only homes most of them had ever known, went up in flames.

After the initial confusion, despair and outrage, Nayukpu and her family, along with others, began the long walk westward away from their burned villages. Few knew exactly where they were going or what kind of place it would be. Most agreed—it wouldn't compare to what they were leaving behind.

The people walked slowly each day, sunup to sundown, rarely given time to rest. To Nayukpu, it felt as though sadness had settled like a heavy blanket over her family and everyone around them. With heads down, her people were herded against their will toward a doubtful future. Soldiers on horses rode back and forth past them all day long. Most people carried possessions on their backs. Some had carts loaded with goods, small children, and elderly relatives. Teams of horses pulled a few large wagons, but all able-bodied people simply walked.

So far, the weather had held and though there was uncertainty, there was also hope. At night as they camped with their loved ones, there was the illusion of normalcy. Children played games, songs were sung and good food was cooked over the fires.

In the evenings as they sat by the fire, Mother and Grandmother talked of the pottery they would make when they reached their new home.

"The soil may be very different in this place," Mother said. "We'll have to experiment until we learn how to work with the new clay."

"It's a shame we had to leave most of our nice pieces behind." Grandmother's shoulders drooped. "There wasn't room for the jug I'd been working on, the one with the swirling leaf pattern."

Nayukpu spoke up. "That was a beautiful piece, Grand-

123

mother. Maybe you can make one like it when we reach our new home."

"I wonder," her mother asked hesitantly. "Did you pack your first bowl? That one was a special piece. I remember how excited you were when you made it."

Nayukpu shook her head sadly. She clearly remembered the day she'd learned to make her first piece of pottery. It hadn't been beautiful like the ones made by Mother, Grandmother and her aunts. Still, she'd been proud of it.

"Look here, Granddaughter." Grandmother's tired eyes twinkled as she slowly reached inside her bundle. She brought out a dark, grey bowl.

Nayukpu clapped her hands and then reached for it. She turned it round and round, feeling the smooth and irregular shape. Then she hugged the older woman. This made her mother smile. It was the first smile on her mother's lips since she'd stood helpless and watched her home burn to the ground.

Mississippi, 1831 October

Dark, ominous clouds brewed in the west and everyone was relieved to stop traveling mid-afternoon and set up camp early. Men and boys constructed lean-to shelters out of logs and branches. The women and girls built fires and prepared evening meals.

By the time they finished eating, the wind had picked up and embers from the fires swirled high into the air. Families barely had time to duck under their shelters before the sky opened and the heavy rains began. Though the shelters didn't keep them dry, they kept the hardest rainfall from beating down on their blanket-covered forms. The strength of the storm increased and the sky split with bolts of lightning. Deafening thunder crashed overhead. Fani cried out with each loud boom and huddled close between their mother and father. Nayukpu pressed her body into Grandmother's side as they sat together, a blanket draped over them both, waiting for the storm to pass.

Suddenly there was a terrible ripping sound. It was as though boulders crashed down a mountainside, spilling all around. The ground vibrated for several long minutes. Afterward, there was only the rain and the distant rumbling of thunder. People began to shout. Then a wail of despair rose up and broke through the rumbles of the diminishing storm.

Nayukpu and her family listened anxiously in fear as waves of lamenting cries rose and fell. Her uncle appeared at their shelter and beckoned her father to follow him. Shortly, Father returned with bad news.

"An enormous tree fell during the storm. There were shelters built at its base and close by. Many people were crushed. Some are dead and many are badly injured." Father paused and what he said next was barely a whisper. "Eliza and her baby, Wren, were killed."

Nayukpu's mother and grandmother shrieked and fell on each other, weeping loudly. Her cousin Eliza, at seventeen, was just a few years older than her. Nayukpu remembered the celebration in their village when her baby, Wren, was born. She felt a stab in the pit of her stomach as she remembered their joyful faces.

During the remainder of that night, Nayukpu held her little brother close, her arms wrapped tightly around him. She tried to stay calm and comfort his fears, but it was difficult. She fought hard to control her own emotions. Their parents and grandmother had gone into the dark, wet night to help the survivors. She and her brother were alone until dawn.

In the early morning light, the men dug graves in the mud, as women prepared the dead for burial. There was much sorrow all around but the burial ceremony was short and before midday, they were forced to gather their belongings and continue the journey. As they traveled, Nayukpu heard moans of the injured and weeping of the grief-stricken survivors.

Mississippi, 1831 December

It was dark when Nayukpu took her bowl to dip water from the shallow, icy stream close to their camp. Her foot slipped and her thin leather moccasin plunged into the frigid water. She refilled the bowl and hurried back to the warmth of the campfire but already her foot felt frozen, making it difficult to run.

"So clumsy," her mother fussed as she took the bowl from Nayukpu. "Take off that wet shoe and give it to me." She stuck the wet moccasin on the end of a long stick and handed it to Fani. "Here, hold this stick up and away from the flames so it can dry."

The wet leather sizzled and steamed, smelling like burning hair as Fani waved it this way and that.

"Not so close, Fani," Mother exclaimed. Then she took Nayukpu's numb foot in her strong hands and rubbed. Tears of pain filled Nayukpu's eyes as the feeling returned. Finally, when she could wiggle her toes, she stretched her feet toward the fire.

Unfortunately, Fani had waved the stick with her moccasin too close to the fire and before anyone had noticed, it had fallen into the embers. Her mother quickly plucked it out but already, a hole had burned in the sole and the leather had shrunk and hardened.

Grandmother examined it but declared it ruined. Nayukpu glared at Fani but when she spotted tears running down his cheeks, her heart softened for her little brother.

Less than a week later and before dawn, Nayukpu awoke to icy winds blowing in gusts through the single layer of blanket, chilling her to the bone. Fani curled up next to her and tried in vain to get warm. Her father and uncle had already left camp with their blowguns. Hopefully, their hunting would supply enough meat for a warm meal.

Before leaving, Father had built up the fire. But except for the few red coals smoldering in the ashes, it had gone out. Nayukpu sat up and tucked the blanket more tightly around her brother. Quietly, she gathered sticks to pile on the coals. She bent close and blew repeatedly on them until a flicker of yellow caught the sticks. She added more wood to build up the fire and placed a pot filled with icy water in the flames.

"Thank you, daughter, for building the fire," Mother whispered, her teeth chattering. "It's so very cold."

It was unlike her mother to not be the first awake and moving around. It worried her. That was when she noticed beads of sweat on her mother's pale face.

"I'll pour you some tea, Mother. Stay there, under the blanket."

Once the water had heated, Nayukpu took a pinch of dried leaves from a leather pouch and placed them in a cup. She poured the steaming liquid over the leaves and she handed the cup to her mother. Then she reached out to shake her grandmother awake.

"Something is wrong, Grandmother." Her voice caught, making it hard to continue. "I think Mother is ill."

With a start, Grandmother sat up. In a moment she'd covered her daughter with her own blanket and had given Nayukpu orders.

"Go and bring more water from the stream."

Relieved that someone older was now in charge, Nayukpu took her small bowl to fill with water. This frigid water would sooth her mother's burning skin. Deliberately, she had chosen the bowl that meant so much to her. Now she hoped it would bring blessings to her mother. She prayed she would not get the sickness so many in the camp had been afflicted with during the past weeks.

When her mother died a few days later, Nayukpu was inconsolable in her grief. She didn't even feel up to comforting Fani. She dropped back, away from her family and walked alone. Grandmother took over Fani's care, holding his hand and some days even carrying him on her frail and bent back.

Finally, her uncle said to Nayukpu, "Your mother would not want to know you are spending all this time mourning, while her mother must take up your duties as well as her own. It is time to stop crying and think of others."

Nayukpu took a deep breath and looked into the face of her uncle. She could see in his eyes that he also suffered deeply.

Her uncle placed his hands on her shoulders. "You are not the only one experiencing great loss," he said. "Your grandmother needs help and Fani needs his sister."

So she returned to Grandmother's side and the two of

them walked together with Fani between them.

Not long after the death of her mother, Nayukpu noticed Grandmother's breathing had become labored and her skin, fevered. Anxious and worried about her health, Nayukpu fed the older woman the herbal tea she prepared each morning. She took her grandmother's bundle to carry, but along with her own, it proved too much for her. With a heavy heart, Nayukpu had no choice but to discard most of the precious pieces of pottery. Blankets and food were what was now important.

The weather was bitter cold with a mix of snow and ice creating even more hardship on the weary travelers. They were forced to walk all day long with few stops. No matter what Nayukpu did for her grandmother, without rest and warm dry shelter, her help was not enough. The sickness consumed the old woman and one day she stumbled to the ground and couldn't get up. Nayukpu's uncle heard their cries and rushed to pick up his mother. She died in his arms.

The soldiers barely noticed when Nayukpu's small family left the trail. Once again, with heads bowed, they carried a pathetic bundle wrapped in a blanket into the woods alongside the trail. Nayukpu wept bitter tears. Father and Uncle quietly grieved as they dug the grave for her beloved grandmother. It could only be a shallow trench, as the ground was too frozen to dig any deeper. Just as she'd done when they'd buried her mother, Nayukpu tried to help dig the hard soil using her bowl and with each scrape the rim became more chipped.

Looking at it, she remembered the long ago day when she'd made this bowl. The memory was all that kept her going. She wished to honor the most important people in her life. She wanted to give them the dignity of a decent burial but all she could do was offer them her tears.

Mississippi, 1832 January

When the shivering group of Choctaws finally descended into the river valley, two steamboats sat at the docks waiting for the icy river to be passable. A camp had been set up and hundreds of cold and miserable people crowded together as they prepared for passage.

Nayukpu and her family huddled under their thin blankets as they watched the soldiers attempt to keep order. Everyone appeared nervous about boarding the steamboats. Soldiers on foot and on horseback barked commands but no one was in a hurry to climb aboard.

"With the ice and the river so high, it doesn't look safe to get on those boats," Nayukpu muttered as she stared down at the black waters below them. She'd spoken to herself but several women standing on the high riverbank with her nodded in agreement.

Fani clung to her back tighter as he peeked over her shoulder. She could feel the tiny puffs of warm air as he breathed in and out. She tried to slow down her own breathing so he would relax and not be as afraid as she felt.

The group watched for a while, absorbed in their own thoughts and worries. Then, to get out of the spitting snow, Nayukpu took her brother under a lean-to shelter, already crowded with mothers and small children. There was an underlying panic in the voices of those that discussed the journey over the icy water.

"We'll be swept away and the children, too," wailed a young mother as she held a small child in her arms with a baby tied to her back.

"They can't make us get on those boats," a woman complained loudly.

"Yes, they can," murmured another.

Arkansas, 1832 February

In the weeks following the steamboat journey to the north and the arrival on the west side of the river, the weather had grown worse. The temperature was freezing and sleet pelted the travelers as they trudged over the rocky terrain and through the iced-over creeks.

Food was scarce and Nayukpu's father and uncle would disappear for hours or even days, sometimes returning with a rabbit or bird, but often, empty-handed.

Nayukpu was worried about her little brother. As she cradled his small, blanket-wrapped form in her lap one morning, she noticed his breathing was raspy and his forehead, hot to the touch. Her breath quickened and she tugged at his blanket to better cover him. She looked anxiously around to see if anyone else had noticed.

"We're going to look for my father," she told the woman next to her. She stood and picked up her brother. "We haven't seen him since yesterday morning."

Away from the others she dipped her bowl into a partially thawed puddle she found next to a dying fire. She wet the corner of her blanket with the cold water to bathe Fani's hot forehead. He was pale, listless and as light as a baby. Many people had died that week from the disease. She'd heard even of several soldiers dying. She scanned the faces in the crowds, looking for her father and uncle. As she wandered through the throngs of people, she tried not to cry.

"Have you seen Charlie Homma?" she asked one group after another. She walked for what seemed like hours, carrying a limp and increasingly unresponsive Fani in her arms. Where were Father and Uncle? Were they sick?

"Nayukpu, over here." She nearly wept with relief upon hearing the familiar voice. Turning, she finally spotted him. Just inside a copse of trees, Father huddled next to a blanket where a person lay, very still. She hurried over and was shocked when she recognized that person as her uncle.

"He's gone," Father said, his voice flat. Then he saw his son and quickly rose to take him from her. "Not this one, too," he cried with panic in his voice.

"No, Fani is sick but still with us," Nayukpu reassured her grief-stricken father. "But he's so weak he can't eat or drink much of anything."

Tears of frustration and sadness froze on Nayukpu's cheeks as she followed her father away from the others. She knew he would need to bury her mother's brother, but first he would find a safe spot for her to wait with Fani. They didn't want others to know he was sick. The disease was too contagious.

Nayukpu nursed her brother day and night. Father brought water in her bowl for Fani to drink. But the food her father found for them, Fani wouldn't eat. He was so weak he could no longer sit up by himself.

The rest of the party went on without them. Though worried they wouldn't be able to catch up with the others, Nayukpu and her father were more concerned Fani might not survive.

Arkansas, 1832 March

It was cold and rained nearly every day. The creeks were

swollen and rushed like rivers. The people traveled slowly across the waterlogged ground and wagons became stuck and had to be abandoned. Standing water was knee-deep in areas that normally would be high ground.

Nayukpu had lost her remaining moccasin in the sucking mud. By that time, it was so worn out and full of holes, she barely noticed and her feet stayed caked with thick, sticky mud. Fani, still weak from his illness, was also barefoot and had, long ago, stopped complaining.

Her small family was like the others, moving forward, heads drooping like cattle with no interest in where they were going. Each day took them farther away from their home. Exhausted and with the deep feeling of hopelessness, they rarely spoke to one another.

Late one afternoon, the rain finally let up. The bedraggled group set up camp in a soggy meadow. So many people were ill and all were hungry. There was little food and most of that was moldy. Nayukpu's father left to search for wood dry enough for a fire.

As she and Fani waited, a group of young women walked past and she caught a bit of their conversation.

"Well, at least it's something to feed the children. It's better than nothing, I think."

"Those soldiers, I heard they have decent food to eat. But they give us rancid meat and rotted vegetables, if we're lucky. Do they like seeing children and old people die, I wonder?" The bitterness came through in spite of their quiet words.

Nayukpu whispered to Fani, "Stay here, I'm going for food." He didn't answer and her heart gripped with the dread that she might still lose him. She took her humble bowl and followed the women.

A large, subdued group holding a variety of clay and

wooden vessels stood close to a wagon. On the wagon, there were several soldiers with buckets of some kind of watery stew. A man on a horse shouted and waved his arms and although his words meant nothing, his message was clear. The ragged cluster of hungry people quietly formed a line and as each passed by, a soldier would pour a single scoop of corn soup and a bit of meat into the bowls they held up. The meager food filled the bowls but would not fill the ache in their stomachs or in their hearts.

Arkansas, 1832 May

Trees were thick and the air was heavy with humidity as they climbed up and down the rocky hills. Mosquitoes and fleas pestered everyone. The sickness continued to take many lives.

Walking alongside her father and brother, Nayukpu tried to keep her mind off unhappy thoughts. She visualized making pottery and looked inside her memory for all the details her mother and grandmother had taught her. She wanted to remember. It would be up to her to hand down this tradition. She hoped she would become the potter Mother and Grandmother had wished her to be. Maybe someday she would have a daughter to teach. These thoughts helped to pass the time and to give her a reason to keep going.

Nayukpu and her father both got a rash from walking through the thick underbrush. The skin on their arms and legs was red and blistered. Scratching made it worse. After a couple of days of suffering, they came to a muddy stream. Nayukpu took her bowl and filled it with the warm, oozing mud. As she dug it out of the creek bank, she thought of her mother and grandmother. It seemed so long ago when they had gathered the mud from the banks of the creek near their home.

Nayukpu examined the mud carefully. It seemed too full of fine gravel to be good for pot making and she wondered what Grandmother would have said about the quality. She also wondered if she would ever have a home where she could make pots again.

Turning back to the task at hand, she carried the mud to her father. There she patted it on the angry, red welts on him and then on herself. It would soon dry and draw the itch away from their skin. That night they could both have relief and be able to sleep.

Her family finally arrived in a camp close to a narrow river in the new district of Okla Falaya. There, they waited to be enrolled and to receive the promised rations for their new home. Of the personal belongings they'd had at the journey's start, few remained. Most had been lost or discarded with the exception of two blankets, a spoon, cooking pots and the ragged clothes on their backs. But Nayukpu had kept her most precious possessions—the pots made by Mother and Grandmother and her own bowl.

Father didn't stay with Nayukpu and Fani during the day, but in the evening he'd return with news. Each day, she would leave her brother for a short time to go for water and daily rations, but for the most part the two of them stayed on their blanket watching and waiting.

"They say it won't be too long before we can leave this

place," Father told them one evening after they'd been in the camp about a week.

Nayukpu nodded but she barely cared. Her head ached. She was tired in body and in spirit. Since they'd arrived, the rumor had swirled around that soon they would leave this camp and go to their new home. Nayukpu had stopped listening. And besides, when they reached that place, it would never be home. Too much had changed. Too many loved ones gone.

It was time to get in the line for rations and Nayukpu reached to pick up her bowl. A spasm of nausea gripped her, doubling her over. When she stood, she was light-headed, dizzy and her vision blurred. The light disappeared and she tumbled forward. As she fell, it was as if in slow motion.

Mother and Grandmother stood in front of her. They smiled and Nayukpu reached out. It would be so easy to take their hands and go to them. But then she felt the pain on her side as she landed on something hard. She opened her eyes and felt her bowl and Grandmother's pot, both broken underneath her. She felt sick and weak. She wanted to cry. She lay still as Fani whimpered beside her and patted her shoulder.

The vision of Mother and Grandmother rushed back and she knew they wanted her to live and be strong. It was up to her to care for her brother and father in their new home. It was her duty to pass on knowledge the elder women had given her.

"I will make them proud," she whispered softly, getting to her knees. She looked into Fani's eyes and placed her hand on his soft, warm cheek.

With new determination, Nayukpu stood and held her mother's pot close to her heart. The future was uncertain and the journey ahead would continue to be difficult, but they would make this new land their home. She had lost much but she would not be broken. One day, she would teach her daughters and their daughters to be potters. It was her legacy to bestow this knowledge on future Choctaws as it had been bestowed upon her.

Leslie Stall Widener is an illustrator and a writer. She has illustrated for children's school book publishers and magazines. She recently illustrated *Why Would Anyone Wear That?* written by her sister, Celia Stall-Meadows, and *Chukfi Rabbit's Big, Bad Bellyache* by Greg Rodgers. Currently she is working on her first Middle Grade novel. Leslie is a member of the Choctaw Nation of Oklahoma and lives in North Texas.

A STORM BLOWS
THE FAMILY WEST

Curtis Pugh

———————

Families broke apart during the Removal. Children from parents, elders from youths. How do you leave one another behind?

This story is based on federal archive records and oral history accounts captured by a descendant and woven into a complete tale of heartache, frustration, and mud. It takes place after the main body of Removals, showing the challenges of those who tried to remain in their homes.

From the fire hearth of a peaceful home to dwelling on a filthy steamboat, we follow the journey of a young Chahta boy as he finds his way to a new home—and a new identity.

———————

A Storm Blows
the Family West

Curtis Pugh

The wagons started moving again. Twelve-year-old Haksi slogged through the deep mud behind his family's wagon. Churned up by the carts, animals, and people in the line ahead, the mud made walking difficult. It was Haksi's job to lead his mother's big black mare along the winding trail. She was too skittish for tying to the wagon and too valuable to place in the herd driven behind the wagon train. He and his brother, Koi, started out sharing the task of leading the mare, but then Koi had to take over their uncle's job.

The second night on the trail, Uncle Hotabi had gone to a nearby stream for water. Moving in the darkness, he did not see the water moccasin until he felt the bite just above the top of his right shoe. Painful swelling soon made him unable to walk. So it was that Koi inherited his uncle's job.

The young man walked alongside the oxen that pulled their wagon. He guided them with a rope fastened to rings in their noses and prodded them with a long stick when they slowed. Their mother, Aiukli, rode on the wagon seat. A few necessary possessions and a little dried food were in the back along with Uncle Hotabi, who was stretched out in the wagon bed.

Haksi alone was responsible to bring the high-strung big black along. The mare wanted to move fast, perhaps run, and the boy had trouble holding her back. She shied and lunged when a new sound or sight startled her.

As a little boy he had been given the name Haksi. It was not that he could not hear as his name meant, but because he did not listen. His mind was always busy, and questioned things. His world was falling apart. Being forced to leave forever their ancient homeland, Haksi, his mother, uncle, and brother were living on the trail. They must move to a land west of Arkansas. Haksi knew that the season was Macha or "the month of wind" called March by the Americans. His stepfather had told him that and it was the year of our Lord 1838, but the boy did not yet understand how years were numbered.

Koi did not seem so devastated by the changes forced upon them. Four years older than Haksi, Koi was called *panther* because a panther's cry was heard near the cabin the night he was born. It was expected Koi would earn an even better name, one descriptive of his character or accomplishments. Or he might do as many did—take a white man's name instead.

Haksi wished for a name as good as even that of Koi. He felt keenly every Chahta boy's longing. A name was important. It was a compliment or a criticism. He was twelve. He would soon receive his adolescent name. Almost anything was better than *he cannot hear.*

Someday, he vowed, *I will be worthy of a better name. I will!* But he did not say this aloud.

As he trudged through the mud he thought about the cold winter night three months ago. Aiukli, his mother, had called the children together. He would remember her words as long as he lived.

"Children," she began, "We have reached a decision. I want you to listen carefully to your stepfather."

Haksi and Koi sat together near the fire in the cabin. Their stepfather, Dougal McLeod, though a white man, spoke fluently in the Chahta language. He had married Aiukli five years ago, a young widow of those called *limoklasha*. In spite of agency corruption, he was a true friend to the Chahta people. They said, "He is a good man even if he is a white man." But he could not stop the overwhelming flood of land-hungry people demanding their homes.

"First of all, I must tell you I am ashamed of my government. I think you already know that. You have watched me and heard my words these past years. Repeatedly the treaties made with your people have been ignored, broken and set aside. The Chahta lands are being stolen with the tacit approval of everyone from the president to the governor and down to the Indian agent.

"We have seen what is happening here in Mississippi. It has been seven years since the last treaty. Things are worse than before. Wave after wave of *Miliki okla* are moving onto Chahta land. I had thought—had hoped—that because of my work at the government agency I could keep you safe, be able to insure you received land according to the fourteenth article of the treaty. I see now I was wrong. I fear not only that you will be driven off any land we claim for you, but your very lives will be in danger.

"Chahta in this part of Mississippi have been murdered for their land. Many others have been driven out of their own cabins. You children have no future here. You are not citizens of the United States. You have no rights at all! You must leave and go to the new country in the west. There you will have citizenship in the new Choctaw Nation. You have uncles, cousins and two grandmothers already there. Your Uncle Hotabi and your mother will travel with you. After your mother sees you safely settled, she will return to live with me here as she should."

Dougal's words produced stunned silence. The silence of broken hearts. The thought of the family torn apart was unbearably painful. Aiukli sobbed, wrapping her arms around herself. Haksi felt his heart being twisted out of his young chest.

Dougal continued. "I have spoken with one of the Chahta captains who works with the government superintendent S.T. Cross. People from this area are to rendezvous in March to go west. You will go to the same place as our neighbors. One of the captains will come soon with counting sticks so we know the exact day."

Silence prevailed. After a time, Koi said, "All these years you have been a true father to us. We do not want to leave. But we value your advice. Perhaps we should go." Koi thought himself a man. He was hungry for adventure. He relished the idea of seeing new things, new country and new people. He had even talked about wanting to see Texas, and the new land to the west was near Texas.

Haksi asked, "What does Uncle Hotabi say?"

Aiukli answered her youngest son's question. "My brother Hotabi says it is his desire to do his duty as your uncle. He has thought about going west, and he will take us with him. There he will make a home for himself and you with our mother who went west four years ago. There you can have land, raise families, make lives for yourselves. I will go and stay long enough to see you settled safely with your grandmother. Then I can return to my husband with peace of mind."

Haksi croaked out his next words. "What will Grandfather do? I do not want to leave Grandfather!"

Dougal replied, "I have spoken at length with the father of your father. Ahuklitubbee will not go west; at least not now. He says 'perhaps later if things get worse here.' I think he will come to you in the new country, but not now."

Dougal outfitted his wife and stepchildren as best he could for their difficult journey to the west. He was able to provide two stout oxen to pull the wagon, the big black saddle horse for Aiukli's return trip, cooking pots, knives, camping gear, blankets and stout shoes for each of them. He did a bit of haggling with another white man and obtained a sidesaddle for his Aiukli to use on her return ride to him.

As Haksi trudged along the muddy trail, he thought of his family's situation. He had seen big storms that came from the west, forests leveled by the twisting, howling winds. But this storm was different, as if the great white-people-storm from the east was blowing them before it—westward to the unknown. Would they survive?

Late that night, Koi and Haksi sat alone by the fire. Camped on a rare grassy meadow, they were out of the mud for one night at least.

Haksi quietly asked his older brother, "Do you think Uncle Hotabi has taught us enough? Can I earn a better name?"

Koi thought about this a little while, contemplating like a

man. Then he said, "It is the Chahta way. The brother of our mother has taught us well. He taught us to be brave. He told us how he fought alongside Andrew Jackson at the place called *Balbacha Tamaha*. He earned his name there. You will do well if you remember what he—"

"But has he taught us enough?" Haksi repeated. "I do not want to fail. I cannot go through life with Haksi as my name!"

Koi frowned at the interruption, but continued. "He taught us to make bows and arrows, rabbit sticks and blowguns. He taught us to fish. He taught us to be wary of the white man's promises. Remember the treachery of President Jackson? We know how to survive among those like him. We have heard the stories of our people, of brave hunters and warriors of the past."

"But I keep failing and disappointing my mother and Uncle Hotabi—and you!" Haksi blurted. "I keep having trouble with the mare. She almost got away from me today. Mother saw it happen, but said nothing."

"You are too impatient with the mare. She is nervous and high-spirited. The slow pace makes her impatient just as it does you. Try to understand. Speak calmly to her. Keep your mind on what you are doing! You remember how Uncle Hotabi taught you?"

Haksi hung his head. He still couldn't do it right.

On the trail the next day, Haksi hated the almost constant stopping and starting. It frustrated him. He supposed that no one hated it more than he. *Be patient! Study to be responsible!* The words of his uncle came often to mind.

The progress of the long line of wagons, ox carts, horses,

and those walking continued agonizingly slow. They were heading toward the Natchez Road. The people traveled a serpentine route following the ancient game trails as they always had. These narrow trails followed what little high ground there was, but wound ever toward the west. The big Natchez Road would turn southwest toward Natchez. Rumors were bandied about that once they were on the *hina chito*, the big road, they would have easier traveling.

At one stop, Haksi expressed his hope. "I will be glad to get to the big road so we can go faster."

Uncle Hotabi was lying in the wagon, his badly swollen leg stretched out. He called the boy to him. "Haksi, listen to me! You are a disappointment sometimes. Do not listen to rumors! The Natchez Road may be a little better but we shall still have mud and shall continue to move at the pace of a snail."

Haksi sighed. *I must learn patience. I must not listen to rumors. And I will learn. I will earn a good name. I will make my family proud!*

As the family wagon stopped on a rise, Haksi looked toward the front of the line and then toward the back. "Look, Koi!" he called. "There are so many wagons that I cannot see the first one nor the horse herd at the back! We must be in the middle of everyone." There were his people in light farm wagons, soldiers driving army wagons, and teamsters hired to haul food and supplies in their heavy freight wagons.

The wagons bogged down near creeks and swamps. Often it was the heavier army wagons or the freight wagons. Teams of animals had to be unhitched from neighboring wagons and brought to aid the struggling teams harnessed to the mired wagons. Sometimes they were unloaded before they could be freed from the mud. Then more time to reload and tie the loads in place. Still more time for the borrowed teams to be re-hitched. The wagon train could inch forward. Then it began again. And again.

Wheels and axles broke and required mending or replacement. Loads shifted and required setting right. On their fifth day of travel a rear axle broke on one of the teamster's heavily loaded wagons and had to be fitted with a new one. This meant finding a suitable tree, felling and hewing it to the proper shape and length.

As they neared the *Hacha* the creeks were flooded. Before crossing, Uncle Hotabi called to Koi and Haksi, "Boys, I need your help. Haksi, tie the mare well to a stout sapling. Koi, find that length of new rope."

His mind full of questions as ever, Haksi asked, "What do you want the rope for, Uncle?"

"Do as I say," was the reply. From his bed in the back of the wagon, Hotabi instructed them. They tied first the front and then the back of the wagon box to the bolsters of the running gear. "Now the wagon box will not float away in deep water," he explained.

Each day when the wagons stopped just after mid-afternoon, the men, women and children all shared the work involved in making camp. There had to be enough daylight to gather firewood, erect canvas covers and tents, see after the animals, cook food for the evening meal, and do washing when there was sufficient water.

After hurriedly tending their animals, boys old enough to hunt went into the nearby woods looking for game. Haksi and Koi would take their rabbit sticks and their long cane blowguns.

The game they brought in helped to supplement the meager government rations of corn, meal, salt pork and salt. No doubt the fresh meat, shared especially with the old and the sick among them, saved lives that otherwise would have been lost due to hunger.

It was a Chahta custom from time immemorial to rise early and "go to the water" as they called their morning purification. Because the long line often had to camp far from a stream, it was not always possible to bathe. Haksi complained to his mother, "I stink! I have never gone so long without going to the water. I hope the next camp will be near good water. I do not want to stink like an unwashed white man!"

Haksi kept hearing they would make better time when they got to the Natchez Road. He remembered the warning from his uncle about not believing rumors. And the muddy condition they experienced daily made him wonder if any road was not mud, mud, mud.

News passed up and down the line quickly. The Chahta captains expected in the next day or so to reach a ferry crossing on the Hacha.

This was both a sad and exciting time to the twelve-year-old. Each day's journey took him farther and farther from his beloved home—and from his grandfather and Dougal and other relatives. He, like all Chahta, felt deeply they were losing something never to be regained. At the same time, the prospect of crossing this river was exciting because he had never crossed a real river. In fact, he had never seen the Hacha or any river before. It was dangerous, but exhilarating at the same time. As his family neared the river, he spotted the ferryboat. He had never seen such a big, strange-looking flat thing before. The wagons toward the front of the long line were already across. They moved ahead while those still on the near bank took turns boarding the ferry. Somewhere beyond this river lay the Natchez Road.

"Wait until our wagon is completely on the ferry before you bring the mare," Uncle Hotabi called to Haksi.

"*Ome*," was the boy's reply as he positioned her to load. But the mare had other ideas. She did not like the looks of the ferryboat, or the water, or the noise made by the hooves and wagon wheels on the wooden boat. She reared on her hind legs. Haksi held on to the lead rope, but almost lost his footing on the slippery bank. The mare pranced and kicked and bucked. All the while she was refusing to go near the strange thing floating in the water. Haksi felt all eyes were upon him and the mare; certainly those of his family were fastened on him.

Koi had gotten the oxen on the ferry with little trouble. He was standing near the animals, holding their guide rope, and spoke softly to calm them. He could not leave the ferry.

But Aiukli ran to Haksi's rescue and together they calmed the big black down and finally persuaded her to step up on the boat.

"You did well," Koi complimented his younger brother. Haksi muttered, "*Yakoke*," but ducked his head between his shoulders like *luksi*, turtle. He had failed again. He needed help from his mother to do his job! *How will I ever be worthy of a man's name?* Tears stung his eyes while he held tightly to the mare's lead rope as the boat began to move quietly across the river.

Back on the trail, Uncle Hotabi spoke loudly enough for all the family to hear. "It is very sad to see our old country so changed." His voice came from the back of the wagon where he sat. After a pause he continued, "I try not to look, but I cannot help myself. To see the cabins we pass each day breaks my heart. All these places once belonged to our cousins and brothers. This land was full of the Chahta people. Now

Americans have taken everything."

Of the white people they saw along the trail, some were squatters who had taken the land, cabins, gardens and fields from the Chahta. Others probably bought them from a government agent. The whole thing was wrong; heart-breakingly wrong. To force people from their homes—from the land of their ancestors—people who had been loyal friends to the Washington City government.

Whether tears came or not, every Chahta heart on that trail was weeping—bleeding—for the great suffering and loss that was their portion. But they were a determined and resourceful people. They would endure.

The days dragged on. Occasionally part of the long line of wagons was able to pull off the trail onto a grassy natural clearing for the night's stop. What a relief it was to be free from the constant mud of the trail! The people, young and old, gathered around fires after the day's activities.

The teamsters and the soldiers whose supply wagons scattered up and down the line sometimes gathered around their own fires in the same grassy places as the Chahta people. Haksi had never heard such boisterous talk as came from those white men sitting around their fires.

The removal captains visited up and down the line at such times to ask how the people were doing and to answer questions. Around their evening fires, the adults talked of many things while the young children dozed. It seemed every-one shared the same distrust of the white man's government, and anxieties about the future. They certainly all shared the same weariness.

One question was on the minds of many: how would they get across the great river called the Mississippi? None of the people Haksi heard speaking had ever seen a riverboat except the removal captain of their group. He assured them he had not only seen riverboats, but had ridden them several times on previous removal trips. He was a serious man who cared for his people and was faithful in his work. Also, the American superintendent, Captain S.T. Cross, displayed genuine concern for the people. The men assured them that though the river-boats were strange-looking noisy beasts that hissed steam and belched smoke from two tall black chimneys, these boats would take them safely across the great river to the west.

Haksi tried to imagine what these steamboats looked like. Ferryboats were quiet, even the big one on the wide Pearl River. The biggest rope Haksi had ever seen stretched across that river and was used to pull the flat boat back and forth. Their Chahta captain told them the steamboats could travel not only across a river, but up and down it as well. At the back they had a huge wheel like a watermill, but instead of the water turning the wheel, the wheel was turned by the steam engine. This did not mean much to Haksi because he had never seen a mill. He could only imagine it. The captain said the huge wheel splashed in the water and pushed the boat either forward or backward. This was the stuff of nightmares to a small Chahta boy, but Haksi was determined to be brave regardless of what he faced, just like his uncle Hotabi had taught him.

As the talking continued, everyone agreed if they had not traveled slowly and stopped often the elders among them would not have survived. Some were frail, and weakening daily. Bumping and bouncing in the wagons and ox carts was hard for them. These ancient ones were traveling alone; their younger relatives either dead, already in the west, or among those still refusing to go west.

Haksi's mother, Aiukli, and the other women always made sure the old and sick had food to eat and water to drink. But often rations were scarce and sometimes the salt pork was spoiled. If the boys and men had not been successful in hunting, the people would have starved.

Haksi found homesickness to be a terrible, almost constant ache in his heart. He worried about those left behind, still refusing to go. He missed his own family members who stayed behind, especially Grandfather Ahuklitubbee, that grand old warrior-turned-innkeeper. He missed the familiar surroundings, the cabins, the animal sheds, even the garden plot and the corn field where he had worked hard to help bring in the harvest.

He missed it all.

Finally, the wagon train reached the Natchez Road and turned southwest. Disappointment filled those who had hoped things would be easy on that road. Haksi was thankful he had heeded his uncle's wisdom and not listened to the rumors.

The road was wider than the trails they had been traveling, and the ever-constant mud was not so deep because the road followed higher ground. This, however, meant uphill pulls for the teams and sometimes slippery descents on muddy slopes. Some places were wide enough that wagons could pass, but it seemed to Haksi that everyone was going toward Natchez and none toward Nashville in the north.

Haksi's party passed ancient grassy mounds near the road. None were as large as the beloved *Nanih Waiya*, but they spoke to him of the ancient people and the homeland he was leaving. The Chahta, normally a happy people, could not remember the last time they laughed. Haksi could not remember when he was happy. It truly was a trail of tears.

Often, they passed stands along the road. Some of these inns were abandoned and falling down. Tall grass, weeds, and sprouts grew where gardens once flourished. Others had been taken over by Americans; the rightful owners driven off or gone away. A few were operated by Chahta families, usually ones consisting of a white man married to a Chahta woman. Only at these few places did they find words of greeting and well-wishing in their own language. These, too, were sad moments. And moments they were, for the long line kept moving. There was no stopping just to visit.

The Natchez Road crossed many streams; some could be forded, others could not. The time-consuming crossings that utilized small ferries were one source of delay after another.

Finally it was rumored they were near Natchez. Haksi was curious to see such a large town as Natchez for it was the talk of many of the people. But he was not to see that place. Captain Cross ordered the front wagons stopped three miles outside of Natchez. Wagons farther back in the line stopped in the best places they could find. Not only did the townspeople of Natchez not want the Chahta in their town, Cross wanted to keep the peddlers of *miko homa* away from the people for fear some among them would be tempted to drown their pain of body and sorrow of heart in the cheap rotgut. He posted soldiers along the road and instructed them to keep the Chahta people away from town and the Americans away from the Chahta.

After two days' confinement in their roadside camps, the people learned there were no steamboats to be had in Natchez. Whether there were actually none there or their captains simply refused to transport the Chahta people was not clear.

So back the people were forced to go. They had no say in the matter. The wagons turned back; the teamsters, the soldiers, the removal captains, the horse herd and the people. Back up the Natchez Road they must go—back over the same road they had just traversed. Back up past Port Gibson and on past Rocky Spring. There a road turned northward to their new destination: Vicksburg.

Going back more than fifty miles the way they had come was heart-crushing to think about. More than one hundred additional miles of plodding on the muddy roads were added to their overland journey because of this error on the part of the government men. Or was it because the riverboat operators refused to take the Chahta on board? They would never know.

The trip from Natchez to Vicksburg took another week. Haksi and all the people were bone weary and hardly able to keep going, but there was nothing else to do. They had no land. They had no home. The white inhabitants of their homeland would not let them stop. The army would not let them stop. They had to keep moving. Their only hope—their only dim hope—was getting to the western country.

Upon nearing Vicksburg, the people once again camped outside the town for the same reasons as at Natchez.

Thus far on the journey, their zigzag course had followed first the ancient trails and then southward on the Natchez Road. This road actually followed an ancient route used by bison and other large game as well as humans in travel from their homes in the south to the sources of salt in what became Tennessee. From Natchez to Vicksburg, their northward trek once again followed ancient footpaths.

Outside Vicksburg, they learned they were to board one of the fearsome steamboats. They also learned that because the waters were extraordinarily high in Arkansas, Captain Cross had decided they would be taken by riverboat all the way to their new land in the west. Because of this, the Chahta wagons must be left behind at Vicksburg. Captain Cross sent word to the people through the three removal captains that those who had wagons or ox carts must sell them before boarding. New ones were promised in the land to the west. Few believed any promises made by white men.

Obtaining what little money the owners of these conveyances could get, the majority of the wagons were simply abandoned. The loads of the hired wagons were transferred to the deck of the riverboat Erin, the teamsters paid off and dismissed, the army wagons disassembled and loaded for transport to the Army's Fort Coffee in the west.

And so the loading of the steamboat Erin was under way. Haksi stared in amazement a moment before all his attention focused again on the big black mare.

On the foredeck and partway along each side of the boat, large pens had been constructed for the horses and oxen. A passageway was left between these pens to enable crew and passengers to access the gangplanks that swung from spars by a system of ropes and pulleys on the foredeck. This passageway was necessary as the firewood supply for the huge boiler had to be replenished again and again on the trip.

The animals were loaded before the people. Haksi held tight to the black's lead rope, determined to handle the loading without help from his family.

As the horses were led down the gangway, one particularly skittish creature balked, then trembled before he reared and plunged and kicked. His owner was unable to control him. The horse lunged in the direction of the black mare and landed a violent kick on her right foreleg. The crack of a bone snapping resounded. Still panicked, the other horse reared and fell over the side of the gangway.

In spite of Haksi's valiant efforts to control the black mare, she went frantic in her pain and plunged through the broken railing into the shallow water between the Erin and the riverbank.

The big black had to be shot.

This was the horse intended for Aiukli's use to return to her husband, Dougal. How she would return to her husband they did not know, but there was nothing to be done. She had to see her family safely settled in the new country.

Haksi trembled and cried within himself. Only words of commendation for his efforts from his mother and Uncle Hotabi finally prevailed and he realized they knew he had done his best. He had acted the man and tried to save the mare. Her foreleg was broken and nothing could have saved her.

The Erin was narrow of hull with a wide overhanging deck that was mostly open to the elements. Haksi saw that besides the main deck, there was a second—or saloon—deck consisting of cabins for passengers surrounded with a roofed but otherwise open promenade. He had never seen so many doors and glass windows in one place in his entire life. Above that was a third deck called the Texas Deck. It was mostly just a flat uncovered space, but had a few cabins for the boat's captain, the pilots, and the other officers. Perched atop it was the wheelhouse.

Besides the space occupied by the animals, huge stacks of firewood for the boiler were kept on the main deck. The boilers and other machinery necessary for the propulsion of the boat, as well as sleeping quarters for the crew, were housed on this deck. This left little room for the Chahta people and their possessions. The soldiers traveling with the people were housed in cabins on the saloon deck, as was Captain Cross. Thus the people were consigned to the open areas on all three decks.

Buckets were strategically placed on the open deck areas for sanitary purposes, but without regard to modesty. The women provided privacy for their sisters by standing with their backs to the buckets and keeping blankets draped over their shoulders. Both human and animal waste had to be periodically thrown over the sides of the boat as the huge paddles pushed the boat upstream. Haksi wrinkled his nose as he witnessed this. *If these are the ways of the Americans, it is no wonder so many of them smell bad.*

The boat's kitchen staff prepared food for the soldiers, crew and officers, but none for the Chahta. At two places dirt had been placed on the main deck, surrounded by stones. Small cook-fires were built there. This was where the people prepared their rations.

The supply of firewood for the huge boilers had to be replenished frequently. Wood yards were plentiful along the Mississippi River and the stops to "wood up" gave the people a little peace as the Erin lay quiet and still, nosed in against the riverbank. Plantation owners along the big river kept their slaves busy in slack times cutting firewood for the steamers. They stacked it in a convenient place along the riverbank to sell to passing boats.

When there was enough time, the people spread up and down the riverbank in order to "go to the water" and bathe. Often, however, these woodlots were located at or near settlements of white people and at these places the people remained confined on board the Erin. Whatever their reasons, nobody wanted the Chahta.

Word spread on the third day since leaving Vicksburg that they would soon arrive at the mouth of the Arkansas River. Their new homes were to be along the south side of this river. The people crowded along the railings as they neared the long-awaited river. Haksi wondered if they were near their new home, but learned their boat trip had just begun.

Almost two weeks of travel on the crowded, stinking, noisy, slow-moving boat yet remained.

Haksi and Koi, along with the others, were torn between great sadness and great expectancy about their future. The sadness came when they remembered again their old homes, the familiar places they loved, their friends and relatives left behind never to be seen again.

Their Chahta captains had seen some of the country to which they were going and said it contained plentiful game. Much of the land was timber-covered mountains, but there were fertile river and creek bottoms as well—places suitable for gardens, pastures and crops. Haksi could only imagine what a mountain looked like.

Regardless what their new country was like, all the people agreed: it would be good to get off the boat permanently! But at least they were no longer walking through mud, mud, mud.

They had traveled for more than seven long, difficult weeks. Settlements and towns Haksi had never heard of before lay behind them now: Jackson, Port Gibson, Vicksburg, Napoleon, Arkansas Post, Pine Bluff, Little Rock, Ozark, Cadron, and finally Fort Smith. Haksi had seen strange things: stores, saloons, church buildings, two-story houses, and the great Balbacha—the Mississippi River. He had not only seen ferryboats, but had ridden upon them as well as the hissing, shivering, thundering riverboat. He had seen forests, grass-lands, mountains and more Americans than he thought existed.

Finally, they were in the Chahta country in the west.

Haksi and his family arrived at Fort Coffee in what was called the Choctaw Nation. They, along with all the others, stepped off the Erin onto the land that was to be their new home. And what did they do first? They had to start walking again!

Somewhere from deep within these deceived, betrayed, abused and exhausted people, these Chahta summoned enough strength to walk the five or so miles to the agency. Once they arrived, Aiukli filed a claim for her lost mare in hopes of re-imbursement so she could return to her husband soon.

Having heard the Erin sound her whistle as she neared the fort, word spread among those who had come earlier to the new country. Most around the agency lived between there and the *Okahpa okhina* where they stepped ashore. Soon those who disembarked from the Erin were met by group after group of their fellow Chahta come out to help them in whatever way they could. The earlier arrivals were themselves in pitiful con-dition, suffering from poverty and the privations that came with starting life anew in a wilderness, but they were happy to welcome their fellow tribesmen.

It was not possible for Haksi to know what lay ahead in the future, but he was alive, he was young, he was Chahta. He was limoklasha—the people are there—the ancient enduring people.

Uncle Hotabi called Haksi to his side as the family gathered around their campfire that first night.

"You have proven yourself," he said. "You earned a new name—a good name. It is a name of which you can be proud. From now on you will be called *Baii Hikia* because you have stood as a great oak tree stands tall and strong in spite of the raging storm."

At this, great joy mingled in the heart of Haksi with all the uncertainties facing him and his family in this wilderness to which the white-man-storm from the east had driven them.

The white storm had blown almost everything away and had blown him and his small family to the new land. They had survived the storm. Haksi—now called Baii Hikia—was determined to face whatever came his way and make a life for himself in this land. This wilderness. His new home.

AUTHOR'S NOTE

"Captain S.T. Cross removed a party of 177 Choctaws in 1838. They left the rendezvous in Mississippi on March 23 and arrived at Natchez April 17. From Natchez they traveled to Vicksburg and boarded the steamer Erin. They ascended the Mississippi and Arkansas rivers, passing Little Rock on May 8. These Choctaws landed in Indian Territory on May 12, 1838."

(*Indian Removal: The Emigration of the Five Civilized Tribes of Indians*. Grant Foreman. University of Oklahoma Press, Norman)

This story is primarily based on the above record, and family stories.

Curtis Pugh authored the book, *Three Witnesses For The Baptists*, and numerous articles relative to the Bible and Baptist history. A member of the Choctaw Nation of Oklahoma, he is a native of LeFlore County, Oklahoma. After Bible College in Tennessee, he served churches in Kentucky, Colorado and Oklahoma as pastor; then for twenty-six years he labored as a missionary in Canada and Romania.

Never losing his love and appreciation for his Choctaw heritage and family history, Curtis is once again in Oklahoma pursuing writing, both biblical and secular. *A Storm Blows the Family West* is based on his family's history.

MY STORY

GEORGE WASHINGTON CHOATE

Jerry Colby

Even the most prosperous and influential Choctaws felt the pressure to vacate their homelands. Long after the initial three years of the government operated Removal, many Choctaws migrated to the new nation in the west on their own, though often escorted by soldiers. This tells of one such family. The author speaks in the voice of her great-grandfather as he recalls his life story.

My Story
George Washington Choate

Jerry Colby

My name is George Washington Choate. In 1854, when I was thirteen years old, my family was forced to leave our large, prosperous farm near Kosciusko, Mississippi, and go to the Indian Territory west of the Mississippi River.

Our farm was very productive due to the large workforce of family and slaves, and my father's good farming practices. He rotated his crops. They were never the same more than three years in a row. The stalks from corn, cotton, and sorghum cane he plowed back into the field as fertilizer and mulch to hold the moisture. We were on the eastern edge of the hard Mississippi Alluvial Plain, or Delta country.

After the Treaty of Dancing Rabbit Creek was signed with the United States government in 1830, any hope of peace in Mississippi was gone. The only reason my family was allowed to stay so long was because of their prosperity and influence in the area. The sorrow and agonizing had started years before, when the Treaty of Doak's Stand had been signed in 1820. So there had been many years of emotional upheaval and sadness, even for the more influential Choctaws.

Our home, slave quarters and outbuildings were modest but comfortable, as was the Choctaw style. The encroaching whites were desirous of owning such a rich plantation, as it was called due to size and location. Some night raids on stock and attempts at stealing crops such as fruit from our orchards of apples and pears, and hay from the hayfield were threatening, especially for the womenfolk.

Several offers to buy the place were made, much too low a price, but as the harassment increased, my father and older brothers decided to go forth to the newly created Indian Territory and see what the area meant for the Choctaw people looked like.

Around 1850, they went by horseback with pack animals carrying food and needed supplies for shelter. When they returned, my father announced, "We are moving sometime in the near future so we might as well start preparing for it."

Four of my older brothers, with their young families, left within a year.

Escorted by U.S. soldiers, we left in the fall of 1854, after our harvests were partially completed. We had three heavily laden wagons drawn by six oxen each, with some cows and horses driven from behind. Thirteen slaves helped herd and keep the livestock moving. The pigs and chickens were caged on one of the wagons, and household goods and farm equipment were stowed inside others. The family members who could not walk rode on one of the wagons.

I had six older brothers. The four who had gone out earlier

settled down near the Red River in the southern part of the territory set aside for the Choctaws. My father had gone out to the territory a second time the year before to look for a place to settle as many of the tribe had already moved and he was concerned about finding suitable land to raise crops and horses.

His beautiful white horses were highly sought after by the military, and he had sold horses to the U.S. cavalry when in Mississippi. He heard of the cavalry remount station to be opened farther west of the Indian Territory and hoped to continue selling horses to them.

The air was crisp and clear when we sorrowfully left our home. Before many days, the weather changed. We made slow progress with wagons heavily laden, and the oxen plodded steady but slow. Everyone was sad; it was not a happy procession that headed west to cross the Big River—the Mississippi—by ferry to a road going west from Eudora, Arkansas. The ferry was small and crossing took many slow trips and several days. Only one wagon and a few of the large animals could be crowded on for each trip. Some animals were balky and stubborn, but finally all got across with no casualties, thanks to my father's leadership and command. We set up camp on the Arkansas side to feed and shelter the people.

I drove one of the wagons despite my young age. My father rode on horseback out ahead, scouting the way, turning back alongside to encourage all—riders, walkers, drovers and especially the young and the women. He had a good singing voice so sometimes he'd start singing a hymn or a Choctaw song to the great amusement of the children who joined him.

My father chose the southern route as earlier removals had severe weather using the two more northerly routes. But we began to have intermittent rain and that was miserable for animals and humans alike. Progress was very slow as the so-called road was only a track and much pushing, pulling and winching had to be used to keep the wagons moving forward. The women were determined and did well in keeping us all fed and in relatively dry clothing. When feasible, clothes were hung around large bonfires to dry. Someone shot birds—duck and geese—and a deer to keep us supplied with meat. We started out with a large supply of the fall harvest of potatoes, onions, corn, beans, and field peas. We had coffee and my mother favored English tea. There was sugar, flour and we carried our corn grinding rock which was oval shaped about twenty inches long, and a wooden pestle used to grind with in case our corn-meal got wet and spoiled. We had corn cakes everyday for dinner and supper, fried in the huge cast iron skillet, or spider, as we called them because of the three legs. The cows continued to give milk, less on some days than others, but food we did have.

After my first few years at schools home in Mississippi, I had spent a few years on the East Coast at a boarding school. My father commissioned me to keep a daily journal of our travels and this I did each night in one of the wagons by candlelight or by the fire if not raining. I carried some pencils and a pen staff with writing points and ink. I used ink if there was time and room to do it without spilling, as it was precious. I didn't know when or if I'd be able to get more.

"Write carefully, son," my father said, "so I can read what you write. I think it will be very important to our future to have a record of this journey. Be sure you put the weather in each day and the health of us all."

I found I enjoyed doing this and reading it to my father who would nod agreement or make a gentle suggestion. He was a good man, always in charge but kind and fair.

So we progressed west across southern Arkansas north of the Red River as the Red could be treacherous. We made poor progress as rain fell hard on some days; then the sun baked and steamed us dry on others. Some of the people had health problems with colds, coughs, and sore feet being the most common ones. I stayed well as did my two younger sisters who rode most of the time in the wagon with our mother walking alongside. My sisters were good little girls and played with their dolls or sang songs or quietly watched the forest for animals or birds to exclaim about to our mother, speaking Choctaw most of the time, though we spoke good English too.

Near present day Magnolia, we veered north to bypass the Red River and got into the most mountainous land I had ever seen. The going was even slower and more hazardous as the wagons were punished by all the rocks and uneven land. Everyone was weary but our father encouraged and cajoled and prodded but insisted on a full day of rest frequently if weather was good. The men would run and play games and the women looked on, happy to sit and rest.

We got into swampy country with cypress trees and different vegetation. My father said we were nearing the Indian Territory. And finally that day came when we found a better track. Some small farms appeared and Choctaw people came out to greet us. That was a happy day. But we were even happier when a few days later we got to the home of two of my brothers. They had a small log house of two rooms with a dog run between, and made us welcome.

After a few days we started north through mountains to the area where my father meant to settle. Having been revived in spirit and body, we proceeded in better time, and after two weeks, we reached a large open prairie and my father announced, "This is our home!"

It had been almost three months since we left our home in Mississippi. There was great rejoicing and a feast was prepared, as wild turkeys were many. The men cut trees from the surrounding forest to build a stockade fence for our animals and a log home for the people. Other Choctaws came from the area south of us to help, and it took about a month. Our property was huge and went up to the South Canadian river. No one else was living that far north yet.

Our lives settled into a pattern. Crops were planted the next spring and I went back to the East Coast for two more years. When I returned, things were going well. Our home had a room for cooking and eating added to the back of one of the original rooms and the slaves had quarters. A barn had been built as well as a hayshed, well filled with hay from the prairie.

A call went out for volunteers to fight for the newly formed Confederate states and I enlisted. I fought in two battles and was seriously injured so I was sent to the hospital set up at Armstrong Academy. One of my nurses was a beautiful young Choctaw woman from Goodland Academy named Eliza Wade. As soon as I recovered I married her and went home to assume my leadership of the family. Tragedy had touched them in my absence.

My father had been sitting in his rocker reading a newspaper on the front porch of our cabin when he was shot by Cherokee bushwhackers—northern sympathizers. The rest of the family fled immediately out the back way and on across the Red River to Texas until hostilities ended.

When we got back together, minus slaves of course, we built out more on the prairie as our first home had been in the woods. We prospered. Eliza and I had one son and two daughters.

I was elected sheriff of Tobucksy County. Then when

North McAlester was established, I was elected Tobucksy County judge. In the 1890s I was elected to the Choctaw senate and became president, working with my good friend, Green McCurtain, who was the chief of the Choctaw Nation. In 1906, I felt the Choctaws should remain independent and so I voted against joining Oklahoma Territory to become a state. So ended my political life.

And so ends my story—eventful but well lived on the whole.

Jerry Colby graduated from Bacone College in 1941 when it was still an all Native student school. She has told her Choctaw family stories to generations of children, grandchildren and great-grandchildren.

Encouraged by her family, Ms. Colby is preserving these stories through writing. *My Story—George Washington Choate* is her first published piece of fiction based on these stories and records. Ms. Colby lives in Asheville, North Carolina, though she frequently travels with her sister, Ramona Choate Schrader, around the United States to attend special family events in such places as Seattle and Phoenix.

UNDERSTAND

Benjamin Zeller

Disease, frozen swamps and the deaths of family drive a girl to desperation. It takes a new friend with a special perspective to show her a different way.

The winner of the 2013 Choctaw Nation of Oklahoma & Five Civilized Tribes Museum Short Story Contest, *Understand* showcases this young Choctaw author's passion for his past and heritage.

Understand

Benjamin Zeller

We weren't prepared for death.
Really, we weren't prepared for anything. Well, anything like this.

Lake Providence Swamps, Louisiana
Winter, 1831

Another scream pierced the heavy air. Byhalia covered her ears to shut out the wailing and ran harder. Her bare, raw feet crunched on the snow that blanketed the swamp. For what seemed like the hundredth time, Byhalia stumbled and reached out to catch herself. She uncovered her ears, and the screams returned, sending chills up her spine. With every scream that echoed through the cypress trees came the frightening possibility that...

"No." Byhalia grunted.

Pushing the thought out of her mind, she gritted her teeth

and ran on. The going was treacherous, and one unlucky step could break through thin ice, sending her plunging into the swampy waters below.

Byhalia could not have cared less.

She ran until she collapsed. Snow sprayed everywhere, soaking into her tattered deerskin dress and onto her steaming skin. The wailing screams were gone, and Byhalia made no effort to move from her prostrate position in the snow. Swirling sheets of white flakes accumulated on Byhalia, merging her body with the frozen earth.

A swarm of thoughts buzzed in her head, begging her to listen to their whisperings.

What if all my chukachafa *die?*

What if I'm the only one of the okla *left alive?*

What if I *die?*

Thoughts of death and despair continued to flow. Each one was slowly chipping away at her sanity.

Soon, she could take no more. Staggering to her feet, Byhalia stumbled forward until she reached the shelter of an ancient cypress tree. She dropped to the ground, sitting cross-legged in the snow. With a trembling hand, she drew her dead father's hunting knife from its leather sheath on her belt, averting her eyes from her frostbitten fingers and trying to forget that there were only four on her left hand. Byhalia took a deep breath and squeezed her eyes shut, hoping *Chitokaka* would receive her spirit, or at the very least, that *Nalusa Falaya* would not devour her soul.

With that final thought, Byhalia's muscles tensed and she drove the knife toward her pounding chest.

At the same instant, something—or someone—struck her from the side, throwing her to the ground. Byhalia let out one blood-curdling scream and everything went black.

"Now hold still…" A fuzzy voice was saying. "I'm trying to help you here."

Byhalia opened her eyes a crack to see the world a swirling gray and white blur. "Where—" she stopped short as a sharp pain tore through her shoulder. Screaming, she tried to roll away.

Something pinned her to the ground, forcing her to stay. "Hang on, there!" the faraway speaker yelled. "We're almost done." Pressure squeezed her shoulder, like cloth was being tied around it tightly.

Moments later, the burning stopped, leaving only a dull throbbing in its place.

A gentle hand helped her to sit up, supporting her back. "There. Sorry about that. How are you feeling?"

Byhalia blinked. Her eyes focused, and she could make out the lazy drift of thousands of snowflakes. A small glade ringed by cypress trees lay in front of her. Her shoulder still stung, but the rest of her body was freezing.

"Well? Are you feeling better?"

Byhalia started and looked at the figure sitting next to her. "Oh!" She cringed at the harsh sound of her own voice. "Yes. Yes, I am." Grimacing at the throb of her shoulder, she added, "I think."

A grin split the face of the young man beside her. He looked a year or two younger than Byhalia's sixteen, wore ragged deerskin leggings and moccasins, and no shirt. His face was long and gaunt, but his black eyes held a cheerful twinkle.

"Good," he said as he adjusted a lopsided eagle feather that stuck out of his black braid. "You're lucky I happened along when I did, or you probably would have hit your intended target."

Both were quiet for a moment, staring into the snowy glade. The boy cleared his throat loudly as he wiped something on the snow.

"Here," he said, offering Byhalia her father's hunting knife. "I believe this is yours."

"Oh." She accepted the knife awkwardly.

What am I thinking? Byhalia thought. *He saved my life, I should thank him!* Still, part of her wondered if she had really wanted to be saved at that moment.

She was opening her mouth to say something when the boy abruptly spoke.

"What did you think you were going to do there? Commit *ilebi?*"

Byhalia's cheeks burned. "Um…I wasn't really going—" She stopped herself before she lied.

"Wasn't going to…?" he prodded.

Unable to meet his gaze, Byhalia looked away and shrugged. "I just thought that…well, it might be better if I…" Her voice trailed off.

The hand that was supporting her back reached up and patted her shoulder. "No. I understand." Removing his hand, the boy placed it in his lap and gazed out at the swirling snow-flakes. "I've thought the same thing myself these past few moons.

"But, enough of this." He slapped his legs to punctuate his statement. "I'm Nashoba."

Byhalia nodded. "*Halito*, I'm Byhalia."

"And what brings you out in a blizzard while half the okla is dying?"

"That." Byhalia sighed.

"What?" Nashoba raised an eyebrow.

Spreading out her hands, Byhalia explained. "Only my youngest brother is left alive, and that may be short-lived. The—"

Nashoba winced. "Short-lived?"

Byhalia scowled and continued. "The medicine man is trying to heal him, but the cold and fevers may prove beyond his skill. This may be his..." She choked and whispered around the lump in her throat. "...his last night."

"Oh." Nashoba said quietly. "I'm sorry." Gently, he patted Byhalia's knee. "Again, I know how you feel."

"Thank you, but that really doesn't make it any better."

"I know."

"But how do *you* know how I feel? It's not as if *your* whole chukachafa have passed on to *hatak illi shilombish aiasha*."

"Well..." Nashoba hesitated, re-adjusting his eagle feather that had started to slide out of his hair.

Byhalia shot Nashoba a sidelong glance. "Yes?"

"They have," he said flatly.

"What?" Byhalia was taken aback. "But, I thought I was the only one so far to lose this many!"

"You are." Nashoba continued to stare blankly out into the snowy woods. When he did not speak, Byhalia turned toward him with an expectant look. She coughed.

Still without looking at her, Nashoba said, "Yes. I have..." He paused. "Well, I *had* two younger sisters still alive when we started this *okpulo* journey of death and sorrow. Now..."

"They're gone?" Byhalia finished.

He nodded. "One of them is. The other is very near to the end. Unless the medicine man is able to work a miracle, she will die of the fever."

"And your parents and relatives are…where?"

"They all died when one of the white man's plagues swept through our okla two years ago."

"So…why did you and your sisters live?"

"Because," Nashoba answered quietly. "They made me take them away south to live in the Pine Hills in an attempt to escape the plague."

"And it worked?" Byhalia leaned closer so she could catch his answer.

"No. It didn't. We all died in the hills."

"What?" Byhalia jerked her head back.

Laughing, Nashoba grinned at her. "Of course it worked! How else would I be here?"

"Oh." Byhalia was thoroughly confused at his sudden change of attitude. "But, why are you laughing? This really isn't funny, you know. Three-hundred-some Choctaws lost and dying in this okpulo swamp!" An angry edge entered her voice. "Why are you even here? Your only living relative is *dying*!"

Still smiling, Nashoba stood up and brushed the snow off his tattered deerskin leggings. "I came out for a calming walk, and you are lucky that I did." He held out his right hand to Byhalia. "Come on! We should both be getting back."

Byhalia gasped and recoiled from his touch. "What happened to—"

"Oh." Nashoba looked at where his fingers should have been. Instead, there were only five blued, scabbed nubs. "Frostbite." He hurriedly thrust it behind his back. "I didn't mean for you to see that. It's been three weeks, but I'm still getting used to only having one good hand."

Wide-eyed, Byhalia could only stare at him. Her one missing finger suddenly seemed inconsequential. "But how did you—"

Nashoba raised the forefinger on his left hand. "Uh-uh. No questions about the hand, please. I've answered plenty of questions for right now, anyway. Now," he offered his good hand to her. "Let's get up and be off. I don't know about you, but I'm freezing. And, I would rather keep the rest of my appendages attached if I can help it."

Now that she thought about it, Byhalia was shivering intensely. Grabbing his hand, she let him pull her to her feet. "*Yakoke*," she said.

Nashoba nodded and started back through the swamp and cypress trees, following a faint trail of footprints.

"By the way," he said, "I'm sorry about your shoulder. Still, I suppose it is better than the other option."

"It's fine." Byhalia mumbled. *How can he be so happy in the midst of such tragedy?*

Nashoba's footsteps slowed, and he turned his sparkling black eyes on Byhalia. "Are you alright?"

"Hm?" Byhalia returned his gaze.

"I asked if you are alright."

"I just don't understand!"

"Don't understand what?"

"You!" Byhalia gestured to Nashoba, exasperated. "How can you be so…*joyful* while surrounded by death and suffering? You've already lost your hand, most of your chukachafa, and now you're about to lose your only sister! I'm quite sure I would have died by now, if I were you."

Nashoba shrugged. "Well, part of it is that I don't let thoughts of despair take root in my mind, or else Nalusa Falaya will eat my soul." He looked hard at Byhalia. "You do know that, don't you?"

"Of course!" Byhalia tried to sound nonchalant. "Everyone knows that."

A smile flickered on the corners of Nashoba's cracked lips. "Good. And you asked how I live through all this?"

Byhalia nodded.

"It's simple, really. Through all the okpulo choices I've made, and equally okpulo things that have happened to me, I've always remembered that life is what you make of it. Unfortunate events are bound to happen, but feeling depressed never helped anyone. It's like now: I made the decision to walk to this 'new land' of the Choctaws instead of riding in wagons or boats. I had hoped the benefits the white men provided would allow me to take care of myself and my sisters. Now, I see that it was one of the worst choices I ever made. Nothing will be able to return my sisters to me." He paused for a few moments. "Some would say that your fate is set when you are born. I disagree. Your destiny is yours to make; you just need the courage to face it."

Byhalia nodded, silent. She thought of what he had said, and a small spark of determination and life spread through her shattered heart.

As they came closer to the camp, the screams returned. But this time, Byhalia did not cover her ears.

Nashoba stopped a stone's throw away from the campsite. "Well, here we are," he said cheerfully.

A pit formed in Byhalia's stomach. She started to move toward the medicine man's lean-to.

"Wait." She felt Nashoba's hand on her shoulder. He turned her so she was looking directly into his dark eyes. "I know you're still thinking about what I said, and wrestling with sadness over your loss. But, remember, if you ever need anything, I'll be here for you, as long as I'm alive." He smiled through cracked lips. "Don't lose hope, we'll make it out of this *makali* swamp somehow."

"Yakoke," Byhalia said.

Squeezing her shoulder Nashoba released his grip. As she turned to leave, he whispered after her, "Understand, your life is what you make it, Byhalia."

And for the first time in many moons, Byhalia smiled.

A homeschool senior, **Benjamin Zeller** is a young author with a passion for preserving his Choctaw heritage through his writing. During his high school years, he wrote a fantasy novella, and is in the process of writing a science fiction novel. Benjamin wrote the winning entry—*Understand*—for the Choctaw Nation of Oklahoma & Five Civilized Tribes Museum Short Story Contest in the fall of 2013. Benjamin, a native of Boise, Idaho, who currently lives in Eugene, Oregon, is a member of the Choctaw Nation of Oklahoma.

MORNING CAME

Sarah Elisabeth Sawyer with Lynda Kay Sawyer

To everything there is a season,
A time for every purpose under heaven:

A time to be born, And a time to die;
A time to plant, And a time to pluck what is planted;
A time to kill, And a time to heal;
A time to break down, And a time to build up;
A time to weep, And a time to laugh;
A time to mourn, And a time to dance;
A time to cast away stones,
And a time to gather stones;
A time to embrace, And a time to refrain from embracing;
A time to gain, And a time to lose;
A time to keep, And a time to throw away;
A time to tear, And a time to sew;
A time to keep silence, And a time to speak;
A time to love, And a time to hate;
A time of war, And a time of peace.

He has made everything beautiful in its time.

Ecclesiastes 3:1-8, 3:11

Morning Came

Sarah Elisabeth Sawyer
with Lynda Kay Sawyer

The dozen roses still have a journey to make after they leave the store today. First, they ride on my lap in the passenger seat while my mama drives. They go with us into our favorite Chinese buffet, since we can't leave them to swelter in the hundred degree end-of-a-Texas-summer weather. As we are seated, customers inconspicuously admire the gorgeous bouquet, soundlessly asking the question: *What is a twenty-something young woman doing with roses? Who are they for?*

I silently reply, *These are for my daddy.*

The roses, still wrapped in their cellophane protection, lay undisturbed beside me in the booth while we eat and catch up on the latest world disasters flashing over the news.

We load back into the car for a short ride on farm-to-market roads until we pull onto a county road and up to a chain link gate. We park and carry the roses through. Up the asphalt road, turn right, then left and down near the cattle pasture. That's what his headstone faces in the quiet country cemetery.

The loblolly pine garland across the half-boulder headstone needs trimming of faded pieces. My mama works on it while I hold the roses, occasionally dancing with a fire ant that makes its way across my sandal. The trimming takes time, but even with the sun blazing down with final fury before evening can arrive, we don't hurry. This time is sacred, a mark of one year following my daddy's passing.

After the hidden wires on the greenery are adjusted, my mama sets to work with her arrangement talents. One by one, I hand her the rose she wants. Largest three in the center, the others making a cascade down each side of the boulder headstone. Beauty unfolds.

Time passes. We have a worship service to go to. But I think of the Choctaws. *Chahta siah hoke.* I am Choctaw. Like many native people, most Choctaws don't live a hurried lifestyle. The joke goes round about *Indian Time.* What it means among our people is that an event begins when all are ready, not when a clock strikes. When preparations are complete, when mourning is done, when the time is right, we begin. Or end.

The roses now arranged, we stand back and admire. We take pictures. Holding hands, my mama prays. Only then can I cry. We cry.

My tears. Her tears. Tears of pain for what we no longer have. Tears of joy for the reunion to come someday. In the right time.

When the time is complete, we gather the refuse and glance back once or twice as we make our way up the asphalt road again.

We are twenty minutes late to the worship service. But really, we are in the right time.

As the sun sets and the day finds a peaceful close, I think of another Choctaw who lost a father long ago. Another who had to discover a time of grief. Just as the above story is based on actual events, so goes the one I am about to tell you.

It is time.

Mississippi. Spring 1834

Who has died? The question beat in Tushpa's mind in rhythm to his steps as he walked with his mother and father to the burial grounds. No word had circulated of a loved one's death among the dozen or so families as they all prepared to march hundreds of miles to a new land. But it seemed necessary to the older ones that they make a visit to the place where the bones of their families rested.

Tushpa's father, Kanchi, led the way as families joined them in the slow walk to the burial grounds. More and more walked alongside him now, until the entire band had joined together as one. And one they must become to survive, his father said.

Finally, the grave houses came into sight, little log structures that covered the resting places of his ancestors. Tushpa glanced around for a new one, the one they'd come to mourn. But instead, the eldest ones of the group formed the inner circle, along with their head chief, Baha. Kanchi joined the second circle and Tushpa found himself on the outer one between his mother and his friend, Ishtaya. The boys had passed only twelve years, not yet near manhood, but they imitated their fathers in front of them, standing tall and somber.

Chief Baha began, and as impossible as it seemed, everything around them fell into greater silence. "We gathered here many times as a people to have a *yaya*, a cry of remembrance when we lost a relative. Now we gather to relieve another kind of grief, the loss of our homeland. We are here to say goodbye to a land which we will see no more."

A murmuring went around, one of such pain that to hold it in would cause a heart to burst. A wail went up from the inner circle, and an old woman moaned, "We are a lost people. A lost people."

Tushpa bowed his head, not strictly from respect, but with thoughts racing as, one by one, each person in the circles before him spoke of the good of their homeland, withholding any evil from their speech. What would he say when his turn came? They were leaving a land they loved. How was a boy supposed to understand so much in so little time? He feared to speak in front of so many.

They hadn't brought food as was customary for a yaya, and Tushpa rubbed his stomach to silence its growl. Something important was taking place this moment, and he could not give in to complaint for food. Still, the growling and hunger pangs continued. And the fear.

His attention peaked when his father lifted his hands and parted his lips, but no words came out. Tushpa held his breath. Though his father kept silent much of the time at gatherings, surely he would not fail to say something to bring honor to them all. But Kanchi said nothing and, after a time, merely dropped his hands to his sides in resignation.

Rivers of words continued round the circle, no one rushed in saying their parting words. His mother spoke hers quietly, the group motionless to hear her grief. When she fell silent, Tushpa knew attention drew to him. Even his friend, Ishtaya, turned slightly, as if wanting direction on what he may say also. Tushpa pulled his head between his shoulders like a *luksi*, a turtle. Something as sacred as this moment deserved great words, but if his own father could not give them, how could he? Finally, Tushpa mumbled just loud enough to be heard by a few, "*Chi hullo li.* I love you."

Nothing noteworthy, nothing deserving of the nods around the circles. Ishtaya commended with, "*Ome.*"

The time for the cry ended.

Night came.

After hastened preparations, Tushpa and his parents were among the first families to arrive on the Great River. As temporary camp construction began, Tushpa joined his father, Kanchi, Chief Baha and second chief Halbi who stood on a huge fallen tree near the angry water's edge. He listened silently to their words.

Chief Baha pointed to the center of the river. "That is *Bihi* Island. In my many crossings to visit our brothers near the Big Mound, I have learned all the currents and landing places. That is the place to rest and straighten the cargo if needed. It will be an easy crossing, but we must prepare."

The location chosen for the crossing was at the mouth of Cypress Creek, just south of Friar's Point. The river stretched a mile wide, and the current was stiff. But since it was wider at the mouth of the creek, the current calmed a bit.

Halbi scowled and motioned to the foaming current. "Water is high."

"We will prepare a raft and canoes while we wait."

Tushpa glanced to the forests they'd left behind, wondering

when the rest of the group would join them. Some had grown fainthearted over leaving and had lingered behind. Kanchi voiced his thoughts to Chief Baha. "The others?"

For the first time, the chief's shoulders hunched slightly. "They will come. Even if we had not given our word, the white man will not let them stay. They will force them to leave."

Not wanting to hear the sadness in the chief's voice, Tushpa scurried away to the camp, putting his youthful energy into helping erect a shelter for his mother. It didn't take long, since his friend, Ishtaya, joined him and soon the boys were left with little to do. But a cheery voice called to them.

"Time's a wasting. You loafers come help me with this canoe."

Tushpa and Ishtaya bounded to the side of Tushpatubbee, the man who would serve as a scout, road maker and camp builder for the long journey ahead. Tushpatubbee stood beside a recently felled tree, ax in hand. He was a man of the woods, with no family to account to. Tushpa admired everything about him, from his coonskin cap and hunting coat with colorful yarn woven in, to his beaded shot pouch and buckskin britches with fringe.

Over the next several hours, Tushpatubbee had them working on the canoe, while dozens of the other men worked on three more. Soon, he turned the work of this one over to them saying, "You're man enough."

This adage was somewhat spoiled when they were joined by an enthusiastic Chilita, the wise daughter of Halbi. While her father erected their shelter, she chose to help with the boat preparation. She was a good friend, so Tushpa hid his frown at the intrusion while Tushpatubbee chuckled and Ishtaya smiled shyly.

Night came.

More of the group straggled in throughout the next day, some bemoaning their losses as evening fell. Whispers of returning to their homes were circulating when a runner bounded into the light of the cooking fires. The young man bent over double in front of Chief Baha, gasping for breath. "Fires. Fire, they are burning our homes. Families…escape. Not all."

A wail sounded, and a warrior stomped his foot repeatedly. "Vengeance!" He drew his hunting knife and sliced the air. Others joined him, the noise escalating throughout the camp.

"Vengeance, vengeance, vengeance!"

Chief Baha's shoulders slumped again. Tushpatubbee removed his coonskin cap and bowed his head, as if helpless to comfort the passing of a life. Halbi, second chief and Chilita's father, raised his knife with the others.

A panic rose in Tushpa's throat. Ishtaya stepped closer to him, as though again looking for guidance. Chilita stood on his other side, the three having halted from their work on the canoe. She stared at her father, then gripped Tushpa's arm, her fear translating to him. She whispered to the boys, "They will be killed. Someone must do something."

Someone did. Someone stepped fully into the light of the cooking fires. Attention drew to him. He raised his arms, and suddenly, Tushpa remembered. Last harvest. It was after his father had gone to a meeting. A missionary meeting. But he had never spoken of it. Just raised his arms as though imitating someone.

Now he spoke. All listened.

"My kin and blood brothers, I know how you feel about what has happened to you, to us as a people. I too have felt the same and looked for comfort from this wretchedness into which we have been brought."

Kanchi's voice boomed. "The Great Spirit gave us a good land and it pleased our fathers to live in it for many years in peace. They loved their homes and so did we, their children and heirs. We lived strictly according to the customs and traditions of our ancestors. They prospered and we thought to have enjoyed the same happy lives, but no, there has come a change and we are in much distress."

Tushpa stared as his father dropped his arms, but kept the strength in his words, shoulders straight, head high.

"Why are we surrounded by foes and cast out of our homes? I have thought much about it and I can see only one thing wrong. We must not have pleased the Great Spirit, and if we did not, in what way did we not please him? It must be in only one way, and in a way that is new to us.

"Some time back beyond our old homes I heard a man preach from a book he called *Holisso Holittopa*, a Bible." Pausing, Kanchi opened the pouch that hung around his neck and drew out a small black book. He swept it upward, slicing through the air.

"Although this book was read by a white man, I believe there is something better in it than the way the white man acts."

Murmurings of agreement and discontent flittered about, but the group of nearly one hundred Chahta continued listening.

"This book sets the heart right. I know. It makes a new man if he be red, white, or black."

Though there were no black slaves among them, Tushpa had seen such people in visits to the more wealthy Chahta communities. His father had taught him that all were one people. The blacks. Even the whites. All with one Creator.

Kanchi still held the book aloft. "Let us all take this word and change our hearts so that we forget this great wrong that has been done to us and be better men so that we do not want to kill somebody but want to help them, and we may be better men than we have in this country.

"Maybe we need to do a good to somebody in that new country, and we cannot do this if we go with a butcher knife in one hand and a musket in the other hand like we used to do. We must change our way and live for love of somebody from our hearts."

Lifting his hands again as if the missionary, Kanchi clutched the book and called out, "Those who want to change, to do better, lift your hands without weapons. Stand. Stand now!"

Knives slid back into the pouches. Almost the entire assembly stood with raised hands, including Baha and Tushpatubbee. Chilita released the hold she had on Tushpa's arm and raised hers. Tushpa raised his. Ishtaya lifted both hands high in the air.

Kanchi shouted to the darkened sky, "The Great Spirit of our Forefathers, look down in pity on us today. We have been a hard, cruel, revengeful race of men. We thought it was right. But today we want to do different. Help us to forget these hard ways and live better lives. We are in much trouble now, but don't want to kill or destroy, so give us hearts that we hear about in this book and let us be good, and if we live to see this new country to which we travel, help some of us to do good to those we meet. Perhaps we will not bring shame upon the land."

Kanchi dropped his arms and nodded in dismissal. Quiet conversations began. Tushpa looked up to meet the eyes of his father who approached him. Kanchi offered the book to him.

"Protect it as you would our seed corn. We must have both to survive."

Tushpa swallowed the last of his fear and nodded, taking the book carefully in his hands. His father said nothing more as he turned his attention to Chief Baha, who was speaking with Tushpatubbee and the other men.

Chief Baha said, "We have nothing to return to. We cannot move forward until the river's wrath lessens. But this time cannot be wasted. We must move with haste until we reach our new land."

Tushpatubbee drew his long hunting knife from its pouch and a plug of homemade tobacco from a pocket inside his jacket. He sliced off pieces and offered them around. "I already got little canoes in the making. How many will you need?"

Chief Baha didn't hesitate in his answer. "Four large enough for four men each. They will pull a raft across the river with the supplies and as many of us as it will carry. Many trips will need to be made. It will take days."

Tushpatubbee spat a stream of brown juice to the ground. "You need a raft too, then?" he asked matter-of-fact.

"Yes. One strong enough not to break apart in the current. We do not want the crossing to be of greater danger than what we are leaving behind."

As if spurred by the urgency of the chief's words, Ishtaya turned back to work on the canoe, but Tushpa stood still a moment. He fingered the pages of the book, examining them in the light of the cook fire some distance away. Chilita leaned over his arm on tiptoe. "What does it say?"

Tushpa shrugged. "I cannot read much of it. My mother went to the mission school but it was so long ago, she only remembers enough to teach me a little. Someday I will learn."

"Me too." Chilita touched the pages as though they were

sacred. Tushpa wondered if they were, so he carefully wrapped the book in a strip of cloth and tucked it into his leather bag.

As the three friends worked, Ishtaya broke the silence by voicing the question they all had. "What should we do about what Kanchi said? How do we please the Great Spirit?"

Chilita brushed back strands that had escaped her folded hair. "We do good. Not only for each other, but for our enemies. We love everyone."

Tushpa frowned, a sudden bitterness rising up as he bent over and continued hollowing the canoe with his iron adze. He punctuated his words with each whack. "How can you love someone who burns your home? Are there any whites who are good enough they would do that?"

Instead of answering, Chilita looked at Ishtaya. "Do you love our people, Ishtaya?"

He nodded, not looking at her as he furiously hacked away at the inside of the canoe.

She poked Tushpa's shoulder. "All people love their own. There is nothing pleasing in that. But when you love someone not your own, or who has harmed you, how can that not be pleasing to the Great Spirit? Is that not what your father said is in this book? Did he not say it speaks of better things than what the white man does?"

The bag lay near his foot. Tushpa nudged it with his bare toe. "But it is hard to do."

Chilita lifted the bag and held it in front of her friends. "But this book tells us how. We must study it. We must know."

Tushpa shrugged. "Perhaps we will someday. If the white men do not attack us first."

More quietly, Ishtaya added, "And if we survive the crossing of the great river." He was looking at Chilita.

Night came.

Days passed, then weeks. The canoes were built, log raft constructed, but still the river's wrath had not completely calmed. The water levels receded, showing a rough path across it, strewn with swirling tree branches and sunken logs. Then the announcement spread through camp like the morning light: tomorrow, they would cross the river.

Tushpa worked alongside the men as quick preparations were made for the crossing. As the head chief had arranged, four canoes with sixteen men would tow the sizable raft load by load, until all of their clothing, household goods, provisions and people made it safely to the other side. His father, Kanchi, was tying down the seed corn on the raft, as it would make the voyage first in the morning. Tushpa held the load from shifting while his father tightened the ropes. When they finished, Kanchi nodded to his son. "Remember, protect the book as we protect the seed corn. Without them, we cannot begin a pleasing life to the Great Spirit when we reach the new land."

Tushpa touched the leather bag that had hung around his neck since the night his father had calmed, then revived the spirits of their people. "I will. Then you will teach us more, won't you?"

Kanchi smiled, a rare sight. "The Great Spirit will teach us all in His own way. His Son..." Kanchi paused, struggling to find the right words. Then he shrugged. "You will understand."

Tushpa just nodded in respect, turning to help Tushpa-tubbee carry one of the canoes close to the water's edge.

Night came.

Joy mingled with sorrow, despair with hope, excitement with fear as the small band of Chahta scurried the next morning and the river crossing was under way. The young children laughed and played and sang with happiness at the grand adventure ahead. The old people lamented the departure from their homelands, and wondered if they would survive to see the new. Tushpa felt himself in between the old and the young. He stood with Ishtaya and Chilita, the three friends in thoughtful quietness as they stood at the foamy edge of the river.

Tushpatubbee launched in the first canoe with his paddle mates, and the other three canoes followed suit. Lastly, eight men gave the previously anchored raft a shove into the current. A few gasps sounded from the three women and five children aboard. Chief Baha stood guard on the back of the raft, his voice soothing as the river took partial command of their craft. It rocked a moment, then jerked as the ropes from the canoes tightened and forced it to follow behind them. Finally, it and the river accepted the fact that the raft was crossing to the other side, into a new reality.

Tushpa breathed, and Chilita sighed in relief. Ishtaya said, "So many trips to make."

When the first party reached midpoint across the wide river, Tushpa watched as the canoes landed on what Chief Baha had called Bihi Island. The men hauled on the ropes until the raft was securely clear of the swift current. Tushpa couldn't tell what they were doing, but the chief had said the island was the place where they would land if any cargo needed adjusting before making the second half of the trip.

Those on the bank near Tushpa crowded closer to the edge, some squinting and whispering. One old woman wiped her eyes in an effort to see clearer. Then a figure near the canoes stood tall and waved. Even from this distance, Tushpa could see the full grin on Tushpatubbee's face, and he knew everything was all right. Kanchi assured those who watched by saying, "We are strong. We have good leaders. We will make it through this journey with the help of the Great Spirit. We will become a better people."

Murmurs of agreement went around.

After some time had passed, the canoes launched again, towing the raft behind them. It didn't take quite as long for the party to reach the far bank as it had the island. The first half of the crossing was more treacherous than the second.

More time was taken as the raft was unloaded on the far side and launched once again for the near bank. Tushpa shifted his foot and worried over how long it would take before all crossed. They had started earlier, and Chief Baha was optimistic over completing it in a few days, but Tushpa worried still.

After several more loads, the raft was being towed back when Tushpa felt a hand on his shoulder. He had sat in the grass away from the remaining group, content with watching the proceedings since his help wasn't needed. Now he looked up at his father, who had already taken more than one turn in paddling the canoes. His face looked tired, but his eyes shone. "You will cross on this trip with your mother."

Tushpa jumped to his feet, suddenly excited to finally cross the river after watching four other trips. But his father kept a stilling hand on his shoulder. "The river is not under our control. We are at its mercy. But we are more at the mercy of the Great Spirit no matter what we face in this journey. Remember this."

Anxious to get the last of his things, Tushpa hurried a nod and bounded off. He was glad to see his friends Ishtaya and Chilita gathering with their mothers as their fathers met the canoes just landing. They would cross together.

It took longer than Tushpa wanted for the raft to be loaded. But with each trip, the men took great care in arranging things so that the women and children and old could ride comfortably on the rippling water.

At last, it was time to board. Tushpa helped his mother climb on before scrambling near the front of the raft where he could see the canoes. Tushpatubbee, Halbi, and Chief Baha were all among those who would help tow on this trip. Glancing around, Tushpa saw his father take position as guard on the back, and Chilita and Ishtaya climbed around the sacks of clothing and blankets to join Tushpa. A mother with two small children huddled near Kanchi.

A whoop from Tushpatubbee and the raft jerked out into the current. Chilita released a small gasp and Ishtaya slid a little closer to her. Tushpa lifted up on his knees to spot Bihi Island. Suddenly, it seemed farther away than it had from the bank.

The river grumbled and complained beneath them, but didn't toss them about as it had some of the trips. Tushpa felt the rhythm glide up through his body, the gentle rocking of the raft a strange comfort in midst of the disaster and adventure they found themselves in.

Bihi Island swayed in the distance that was closing with each powerful stroke of the sixteen men in the four canoes. Tushpa relaxed on his heels. They would soon be across and on their way at last to the new home...

"Ay!"

The raft pitched back sharply. Tushpa scrambled for a handhold, looking for his mother and at the same time, discovering the cause of the shift. A swiftly moving tree, mostly submerged, had swirled and slammed into one corner of the raft, sinking it.

Unable to grab onto anything, Tushpa tumbled into the

frigid river. His head surfaced almost immediately, a scream he didn't recognize as his own flying from his lips. He shook the water from his eyes and tried to swim, but where? How? Each handful of water he reached for entangled him with the blankets as the river took command of his body. He was at its mercy.

No. You are at the mercy of the Great Spirit. He wants you. He is with you.

His father's voice mixed with one he believed he should know but didn't recognize blended with screams in the water around him. Twisting, Tushpa caught sight of his father balancing the raft while at the same time pulling his mother on, and Ishtaya's mother, and the mother of the two other children. How could he do it all at once? Then Kanchi looked around, and Tushpa knew his father's searching gaze. He was too far in front of the raft for his father to see him. He tried to call out, but water replaced his words.

The two little children cried out, splashing near the back of the raft. Kanchi dove in by them, scooping one in his arm while the other latched onto his long hair. He used his powerful free arm to paddle close enough to the raft for the mothers to grab the children.

With a soggy blanket wrapped around one arm and body overcome with shivers, Tushpa suddenly lost the strength to keep himself above water. He gripped the leather pouch still around his neck as he went under. At the same time, a rough hand grabbed the back of his neck. He was hauled up and over the uneven edge of a canoe. Someone briskly rubbed his chest. Tushpa took a breath and opened his eyes to stare at Tushpatubbee.

He coughed, vaguely aware of his mother's scream. He tried to answer her. *I'm alive, I'm alive,* he wanted to say but no words came out. Tushpatubbee wasn't looking at him. His eyes scanned the waters out of Tushpa's sight as he lay in the bottom of the canoe. The men above him looked like giants. Their gazes were fierce as they started paddling again. But it seemed to Tushpa they were going in a circle and not even pulling the raft.

Tushpatubbee threw his paddle down by Tushpa's head before diving into the water.

Chilita? Ishtaya?

With a shout, Tushpa sat up and tried to locate his friends. Dizziness made it several seconds before he could see the raft clearly. Then he spotted them. Chilita, Ishtaya, their mothers, the two children. All safely aboard the balanced raft.

Then why were Tushpatubbee and two other men being tossed about in the river, searching the angry waters? Surely, they could pull the blankets in without...

Tushpa's heart stilled, his breath stuck to his cold lips. Kanchi. His father!

His mother wailed, being held in place by Chilita's mother. Ishtaya looked at Tushpa, then away.

The gentle rocking was no longer a comfort. It was a mockery. It whispered that even when things are peaceful, evil lurks beneath it.

Tushpatubbee had regained his place in the canoe, silently paddling with his back to Tushpa, his shoulders hunched. Tushpa didn't move, didn't speak as the little band struggled on to Bihi Island. He sat in the bottom of the canoe, legs crossed, hands on his knees, staring out into the waters, waiting. Waiting for his father to surface, for the defeated words of Chief Baha to not be true. *He was tangled in the branch. We have done all we can to find him. He is no longer with us.*

The canoe dragged through the muddy bottom that surrounded the island as it made a forceful slide onto its bank. The four men piled out and dragged the canoe on shore, then turned and hauled the shaking raft in. Tushpa stayed seated in the canoe, watching. The men helped everyone off the raft, checking for injuries and offering what little comfort they could after the ordeal. His mother was no longer crying. She simply held herself and stared over the river passage they'd just made. Waiting. Watching.

Chilita held her mother's hand, Ishtaya slipped away from them and came to Tushpa. He knelt by the canoe, bringing them eye level, but he didn't look at him. Just put a hand on the rim and stared over the waters. Somehow, they seemed calmer now.

Chief Baha's shoulders slumped. "I should not have let him make the crossing so many times. It weakened him."

A wail sounded from the mother of the small children. She gripped the dripping wet young ones in her arms and cried. "Why go on?" she moaned. "Why go on?"

Tushpatubbee hung his head, scrubbed his hands over his face. "I couldn't find him. Tried. Tried hard." He looked to the river. "He was a great leader. Don't know what we can do now."

Tushpa gripped his knees harder, then released them. His father had given him a charge before the crossing. Now was the time.

Both hands on the pouch that had survived the dunk in the river, he stood and stepped out of the canoe. He carefully withdrew the dampened book and held it up as his father had. "We must go on to honor my father and the truth he brought to us. The Great Spirit has given us a guide. He will be with us now, though my father cannot." Tushpa swallowed as faces turned to him, ones filled with despair, fear, fatigue. "Remember the prayer he made for us, that we may become a better people. We can only do that with the help of the Great Spirit. And His Son." With the last word spoken aloud, Tushpa understood. He couldn't explain, but he knew. Someday, he would tell them all what he understood.

He brought the book down to his chest and bowed his head, unsure what else to say. But Ishtaya rose and said, "Ome."

Chilita released her mother's hand and came to them, tears still in her eyes. "We will study this book. We will help our people."

Tushpatubbee stepped closer and asked, "Will you pray for us like your father did?"

Stunned, Tushpa clenched the book tighter. He glanced back to the waters, but he knew. His father was gone. He stood in his place now. The Great Spirit had passed the burden to him, and would give him the strength to carry it.

Lifting hands high with the book, Tushpa prayed. "Great Spirit, hear our cries. We are a lost people, a people without hope outside of You. Make us better. Help us understand this book You gave us. Help us get to our new land. Help us to do good there so that the ones who will live on many years from now may prosper and hope in You." He lowered his arms, still holding the book in front of him. He glanced to each side to include his two friends. "Those who want to study this book with us, step forward."

Tushpatubbee put a hand on his shoulder and squeezed. Chief Baha moved closer to them, as did the mother with two young ones in tow. "He sacrificed his life to save my children," she said, arms wrapped around them, hands on their chests.

Most of the canoe paddlers stepped forward. Others

pretended to busy themselves with adjusting the raft for the remaining journey, including Chilita's father, Halbi. Her mother shifted her feet, looking between her daughter and husband. Ishtaya's mother stepped forward. "He showed how the Great Spirit wants us to love. We must become worthy of that."

Tushpa's mother walked up to him and put a strangely warm hand on his cheek. She said nothing with her lips, only her eyes. Then she dropped her hand and glanced out at the river one last time before turning away.

Soon, the worn party reloaded for the second half of the crossing. Tushpa would never forget what had happened that day, never forget his father's death or the transfer of responsibility for his people. He felt the love of the Great Spirit in his heart. But they still had a long way to go.

Night came.

After a week of hard work, the crossing was complete with no further tragedies. The party decided to rest a few days before continuing the westward journey, and made a temporary camp on the high ground away from the riverbank. It had been weeks since they'd left their homes, and the fatigue led to sickness among the group. But Tushpa still made his request to Chief Baha. The next day, the entire assembly gathered on the riverbanks for a special yaya.

This time, it was Tushpa in the inner circle, next to his mother who had covered her head with a cloth. Ishtaya and Chilita, along with their mothers, gathered near, being their most intimate friends. Tushpatubbee stood behind Tushpa. All heads were draped with cloths and each person began muttering some expression of sorrow or extolled the good qualities of

Kanchi, though his name was not spoken.

The sun was at high noon when they began, but the ceremony went on, with occasional breaks to eat. Finally, the group grew quiet, but no one left. Tushpa understood. They were waiting for him to give the final words at his father's grave, words of great meaning and encouragement. Tushpa lifted his eyes to the river waters as the sun cast its final glow upon them. He said the words that seemed right, without fear.

"Chi hullo li. I love you."

Ishtaya said, "Ome."

Night came.

Before dawn the next morning, Tushpa crept back to the river's edge, the book tucked under his arm. It had dried, only a few pages lost to tears and running lines.

He sat on a boulder and stared over the waters, grief filling him as tears he'd held back, came. How could he cry in front of those who looked to him for spiritual guidance? He did not know much about the book. But neither had his father, yet he shared what he had. Maybe that's all Tushpa needed to do. Share what he had, what he'd been given.

Lifting the book once again, Tushpa said, "Ome. It is so."

So much darkness and evil had already befallen them. But as the first rays of the sunrise spilled over the water, it reminded him there was much light ahead. It was time.

Morning came.

AUTHOR'S NOTE

This story is based on a manuscript written by James Culberson, the son of Tushpa. His final line reads: "And who on his [Tushpa's] deathbed enjoined me to keep the family together and give them a chance for an education; to be a good citizen, and write the history of the journey if I thought it a benefit to mankind."

————————

Sarah Elisabeth Sawyer is an award-winning author and a Choctaw storyteller of traditional and fictional tales based on the lives of her people. In 2012, she was honored as one of four artists in the Smithsonian's National Museum of the American Indian Artist Leadership Program for her literary work in preserving Trail of Tears stories. A regular columnist in Book Fun Magazine and the Northeast Texan, she writes from her hometown in East Texas.

Lynda Kay Sawyer focuses on the research and filmmaking aspect of the Sawyer mother and daughter team. For her most recent project, she produced a promotional video for the Smithsonian's National Museum of the American Indian. Lynda Kay is currently working on a screenplay based on her Choctaw family history.

————————

GLOSSARY OF CHOCTAW WORDS

The Choctaw people have spoken their language for unknown decades, but dialects and translations can vary from district to district and generation to generation. Some of the words used in this book were interpreted through the Choctaw Nation of Oklahoma Language Department while others came from sources such as the writings of Peter J. Hudson (Choctaw). We strive for accuracy on all fronts, but ultimately had to make choices for use in our stories.

Ahuklitubbee: To catch him and to kill him.

Aiukli: Beautiful

Baii Hikia: Oak tree that stands upright as a man.

Balbacha: The Chahta name for the Mississippi River.

Balbacha Tamaha: Tamaha means town. Together with the name of the river this was the Chahta name for New Orleans.

Bihi: Mulberry

Byhalia: White oaks

Chahta: Choctaw. Also spelled Chahta, Chactas, Tchakta, Chocktaw, and Chactaw

Chahta siah hoke: I am Choctaw.

Chi pisa la chike: I will be seeing you, I will see you later.

Chitokaka: The Great Spirit

Chukachafa: Family

Hacha: Choctaw name for the Pearl River.

Haksi: He cannot hear.

Halito: A friendly greeting.

Hatak illi shilombish aiasha: The afterworld

Hina chito: Big road

Hoke: Used at the end of a statement for emphasis.

Hokli ho: Imperative signal to teammates to seize and hold the nearest opposing player.

Holisso Holittopa: Phrase for the Holy Bible.

Hotabi: To look for and to kill.

Ilebi: Suicide

Nalusa Falaya: The Soul Eater (the devil)

Nanih Waiya: Name of ancient mound in Mississippi sacred to the Choctaws.

Limoklasha: "The people that are there," often appears as *Mogolusha*, an ancient division of the Choctaw confederacy.

Makali: Evil, vile, bad

Luksi: Turtle

Miko homa: "Red Chief," an old Choctaw nickname for whiskey.

Miliki okla: American people—citizens of the United States.

Ofi: Dog

Okahpa okhina: Chahta name for the Arkansas River.

Okla: Tribe or people

Ome: Very well. Yes, as in a ready assent, agreement or acknowledgment.

Okpulo: Bad, or vile

Toli: Stickball game

Yakoke: Thank you

Acknowledgments

The concept for this book emerged through my experience in the Artist Leadership Program at the Smithsonian's National Museum of the American Indian (NMAI). I was awarded a place in the program in the fall of 2012, and was privileged to spend two weeks at the NMAI in Washington, D.C., as I researched the Choctaw Removal period in such places as the NMAI Cultural Resources Center and the museum on the National Mall, Smithsonian Museum Support Center (Anthropology and National Anthropological Archives), the Library of Congress, National Archives and Records Administration, American Art Museum, and the Congressional Cemetery.

A heartfelt thank you to the NMAI for allowing me to touch history, and for your part in making this book a reality. A very special thanks to Keevin Lewis, NMAI Museum Programs Outreach Coordinator, for your dedication to the Artist Leadership Program, and your encouragement to us authors that, "writing is the most important thing Native people need to do."

I want to thank each of the Choctaw authors themselves—Curtis Pugh, Dianna Street, Leslie Widener, James Masters, Francine Locke Bray, Ramona Choate Schrader, Jerry Colby, and Benjamin Zeller. You all put tremendous work, heart and soul into your stories, and were a true pleasure to work with.

Fulcrum Publishing graciously allowed reprints rights for *Rising Fawn and the Fire Mystery*. Special thanks to Charlotte Baron at Fulcrum for patiently working with me on the details of the project and for securing the agreement. This story is a beautiful addition to the collection. To Marilou Awiakta—who so enthusiastically agreed to the deal and served as a source of encouragement throughout the process—*wado*, thank you! And to Beverly Bringle—my research of your family's story led me to you and Rising Fawn. Thank you for your input and for taking the time to do an illustration for the reprint.

An incredible amount of research goes into any writing, but more so when striving for cultural and historical accuracy. We could not have ensured the details of this book without the help of staff within the Choctaw Nation of Oklahoma. Thanks go to:

Dr. Ian Thompson, Tribal Archaeologist and Director of the Historic Preservation Department, for your dedication and patience in answering the flood of questions we inundated you with. You always had the answers we needed. Lillie Roberts, Director of Internet Classes for the Choctaw School of Language, for reading the stories and providing thorough insight into the Choctaw language. Ryan Spring, GIS/GPS Specialist in the Historic Preservation Department, for your study of the Removal Routes and for reviewing those details in our stories. Shelley Garner, Director of the Cultural Affairs & Arts Education Cultural Services, for assistance with the cornhusk dolls. Melissa Jones, Director of Tribal Membership, for assisting with fact checks regarding the tribe today.

Also, thanks to Presley Byington, a traditionalist on the advisory board for the nation, for faithfully reviewing early drafts of each story for cultural accuracies. Your comments and corrections were culture-savers.

And a final thanks to those within our tribe goes to Assistant Chief Gary Batton for supporting my work with Choctaw stories from the beginning, and for your Christian leadership within our tribe. *Yakoke!*

Other tribal members to thank include ones within my immediate family. To my mama, Lynda Kay Sawyer. Words can't touch what you are in my life. This book would not exist without you. To my brother, Doug Davis, for the research you've done and inspiring me to be a better researcher, going for facts over fiction. To my papaw, William Kenneth Odell, for handing down the heritage of our people. *Chi pisa la chike.* I will see you again someday.

To my daddy, who we "adopted" into the Choctaw family. Your passing drives me every day to preserve stories before they are lost forever. *Chi pisa la chike.*

From all the authors, we want to thank our family and friends for their faithful support and encouragement while we locked ourselves down to write, rewrite, rewrite, and rewrite some more. Your understanding and patience did not go unnoticed.

Each story had its own team of support. We want to say special thanks to the following:

Bryant Rickman, owner and breeder of the foundation herds of Choctaw horses, who served as an equine consultant; Arlee Frantz, editor assistant; Dr. Daniel Littlefield, Director of the Sequoyah National Research Center, was a historical consultant and critic; Sandra Riley, Choctaw and Chickasaw genealogical researcher; Vance Trimble, journalist, editor and author of over twelve books and 1960 Pulitzer Prize winner for national reporting; Dora M. Wickson, Choctaw Nation language instructor; Matthew Street, editing assistant; John Ruskey of the Quapaw Canoe Company for his expertise in canoe making and knowledge of the Mississippi River.

Abundant thanks to my friend, author Julie Cantrell. Your passion truly makes me tear up, and your love and support of our Choctaw people in your writing and personal life is inspiring.

Thanks to Rachel Phelps and Mollie Reeder, two excellent writers, for your input on the book. And to Kelly Blanchard, another excellent writer, for graciously allowing me to use her title idea, *Touch My Tears*. It couldn't have been more appropriate.

A beautiful bouquet of thanks to our primary illustrator, Leslie Widener. You captured emotion, drama and culture with your pen.

The cover design was brought to life by our awesome graphic designer, Josh McBride. Thanks for your fabulous work, font choices, and the iris sunrise. You rock. (josh360.com) Oh and of course, special thanks to the handsome model who shaved his month-old beard just for me even though it ended up not necessary—my brother, Jon Sawyer. And to Lynda Kay Sawyer for capturing the awesome shot.

To my critique family, God's Garden Writers. You provided the support and love I needed in the final push toward publication.

To Tim Tingle and Greg Rodgers. You helped me find a voice in writing and telling the stories of our people. *Yakoke*.

Finally, to my Lord and Savior, Jesus Christ. I can do all things through Him, and apart from Him, I am nothing.

—Sarah Elisabeth Sawyer, author, editor

Continue the Journey…

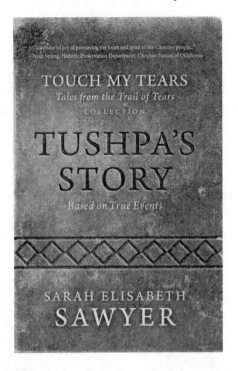

"Protect the book as you do our seed corn. We must have both to survive."

The Treaty of Dancing Rabbit Creek changed everything. The Choctaw Nation could no longer remain in their ancient homelands.

Young Tushpa, his family, and their small band embark on a trail of life and death. More death than life lay ahead.

Tushpa's Story (Touch My Tears Collection) is available on Amazon.com

Choctaw Tribune Series, Book 1

Who would show up for their own execution?

It's 1892, Indian Territory. A war is brewing in the Choctaw Nation as two political parties fight out issues of old and new ways. Caught in the middle is eighteen-year-old Ruth Ann, a Choctaw who doesn't want to see her family killed.

In a small but booming pre-statehood town, her mixed blood family owns a controversial newspaper, the *Choctaw Tribune*. Ruth Ann wants to help spread the word about critical issues but there is danger for a female reporter on all fronts—socially, politically, even physically.

But what is truly worth dying for? This quest leads Ruth Ann and her brother Matthew, the stubborn editor of the fledgling *Choctaw Tribune*, to old Choctaw ways at the farm of a condemned murderer. It also brings them to head on clashes with leading townsmen who want their reports silenced no matter what.

More killings are ahead. Who will survive to know the truth? Will truth survive?

***The Executions* (Choctaw Tribune Series, Book 1) is available on Amazon.com**

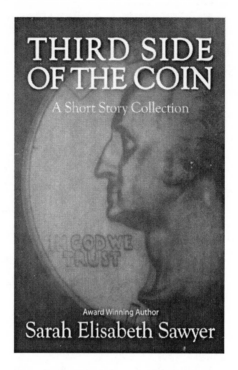

With the gift to find real meaning in a story, author Sarah Elisabeth Sawyer creates tales to stir the heart and evoke deep, often buried emotions. Not one to shy away from tragedy or crisis of faith, she explores human conditions through engaging short stories.

Third Side of the Coin **is available on Amazon.com**

CPSIA information can be obtained
at www.ICGtesting.com
Printed in the USA
FSOW02n1246050517
33934FS